I, Q Series

Book One:
Independence Hall

Book Two:
The White House

Book Three:
Kitty Hawk

Book Four:
The Alamo

I, Q

(Book Four: The Alamo)

Roland Smith

and

Michael P. Spradlin

Sleeping Bear Press

Copyright © 2013 Roland Smith
Copyright © 2013 Michael P. Spradlin

Library of Congress Cataloging-in-Publication Data
Smith, Roland, 1951-
The Alamo / by Roland Smith and Michael P. Spradlin.
pages cm. -- (I, Q ; book four)
Summary: "When Quest (Q) and his stepsister Angela head to
Texas for their parents' concert, they discover traces of the terrorist group
Ghost Cell in the Lone Star state"-Provided by publisher.
ISBN 978-1-58536-822-8 (hard cover) -- ISBN 978-1-58536-821-1 (paperback)
[1. Spies--Fiction. 2. Terrorism--Fiction. 3. Stepfamilies--Fiction. 4.
Musicians--Fiction. 5. Alamo (San Antonio, Tex.)--Fiction. 6. Mystery
and
detective stories.] I. Spradlin, Michael P. II. Title.
PZ7.S65766Al 2013
[Fic]--dc23
2013004284

ISBN 978-1-58536-821-1
1 3 5 7 9 10 8 6 4 2

ISBN 978-1-58536-822-8 (case)
1 3 5 7 9 10 8 6 4 2

This book was typeset in Berthold Baskerville and Datum
Cover design by Lone Wolf Black Sheep
Cover illustration by Kaylee Cornfield

Printed in the United States.

Sleeping Bear Press™

315 E. Eisenhower Parkway, Suite 200
Ann Arbor, Michigan 48108

© 2013 Sleeping Bear Press
visit us at sleepingbearpress.com

*For all my friends, readers, teachers, and librarians
in the great state of Texas.*
–Roland

*For Roland Smith.
Thanks for letting me take the Ferrari for a drive.*
–Mike

Cast of Characters

Quest (Q) Munoz: Q is thirteen and wants to be a famous magician when he grows up. His idol is the great magician Harry Houdini. Q is ambivalent about school, but gets As in math and writing. He is seriously opposed to his new stepfather's vegetarianism and sneaks junk food at any opportunity. Tall with blond hair, he dresses the same way almost every day, usually in some variation of cargo pants or cargo shorts and a polo or T-shirt.

When Q is nervous, he shuffles cards and practices card tricks. It helps him relax and concentrate. He has a complicated relationship with his biological father, Speed Paulsen. Q is prone to premonitions, occasionally feeling that something bad is about to happen. He calls these feelings "the itch." The itch proves useful to Q and Angela on more than one occasion.

Angela Tucker: Angela, fifteen, has shoulder-length black hair with bangs, and olive skin. She has dark brown eyes and, upon first meeting her, Q thinks she is thin and a little frail-looking. But Angela is anything but frail. She wants to be a Secret Service agent like her mother, Malak Tucker, who died in the line of duty. Angela is smart, observant, and highly organized.

Angela always carries a small tattered backpack, in which she keeps extra hats, sunglasses, and other items that help her disguise her appearance when she practices her countersurveillance techniques and tradecraft (a term spies and agents use that refers to the techniques of trailing a suspect, eluding a tail, and other methods they use in performing their duties). Angela keeps her desire to be an agent secret from her father, Roger, who would not approve.

Blaze Munoz and Roger Tucker: Q's mom and Angela's dad have recently married. They are musicians and perform together as the duet Match. After marrying in a ceremony in San Francisco, they take Q and Angela on tour with them across the country.

Tyrone Boone: Boone is an old roadie (someone who travels with musicians and musical acts, performing all kinds of tasks on a tour). Boone is in charge of tour security and keeps an eye on Q and Angela. He travels with his very old, nearly toothless, and quite smelly dog, Croc. Boone is a former NOC (No Official Cover) agent for the CIA. He now uses a network of former spies to run "off-the-books" or unofficial operations.

Malak Tucker: Angela's mother and a United States Secret Service agent.

Eben Lavi: A rogue Mossad agent. (Mossad is roughly the Israeli equivalent of the CIA.) Eben is tracking a terrorist he believes is responsible for his brother's death. He believes the assassin known as "the Leopard" has a connection to Angela.

Ziv: The mysterious Ziv is a NOC agent for Mossad.

Buddy T.: Buddy T. is Blaze and Roger's manager. Though he is obnoxious and offensive in practically every way, he's still one of the most successful managers in the music business. Roger jokes that the "T" stands for "To-Do," because when Buddy talks he sounds like he's giving everyone a "to-do" list.

Dirk Peski: Dirk is nicknamed "the Paparazzi Prince" because he takes photos of the rich and famous and sells them to tabloid newspapers and gossip websites. Dirk is one of Ziv's operatives, or agents.

J. R. Culpepper: J.R. is the president of the United States, or POTUS, as he is referred to by the Secret Service. Before being elected president he served in the U.S. Senate, was vice president, and was director of the CIA.

Marie and Art: Marie and Art are Roger and Blaze's personal assistants, or PAs. Buddy T. thinks that he hired them but in fact they are highly trained agents and bodyguards working for Boone.

Heather Hughes: Heather is the president of a record company and responsible in large part for putting Match back on the charts. She knows Boone well from all her years in the music industry. Mostly her job appears to be keeping Buddy T. mollified and out of everyone's way.

P.K.: P.K. is short for President's Kid, the Secret Service code name for Willingham Culpepper, son of J. R. Culpepper. P.K. is ten years old, but smarter than most and wise beyond his years. He knows the location of many of the secret passages in the White House and has a Secret Service radio, which he uses to keep tabs on the agents so that he can practice eluding them.

Bethany Culpepper: J.R. is widowed and his daughter, Bethany, takes on the role of first lady.

Speed Paulsen: Q's biological father. Speed is a rock star and loves to play the part. He earned the nickname Speed because he could pick guitar faster than anyone alive. It's been a while since Speed has had any hit songs and he is jealous of his ex-wife's sudden, newfound success. Speed is annoying, hapless, confused, in and out of rehab, but at the same time strangely likeable.

Agents Charlie Norton and Pat Callaghan: Secret Service agents whom J.R. assigns to Boone's team. Both men are capable, trustworthy, and devoted to J.R. and his family.

The SOS team: A group of Boone's most trusted operatives. SOS stands for "Some Old Spooks." The team consists of:

X-Ray: The technical genius. He spends most of his time in a beat-up old van the team calls the "intellimobile." There is no computer system and no database or piece of electronic equipment X-Ray cannot hack, master, construct, or duplicate.

Vanessa: The team's designated "world's deadliest old broad." She is a master knife thrower, and Boone refers to her as a "human lie detector" due to her ability to read people and determine if they are telling the truth. Vanessa is also an exceptional driver and adept at tailing suspects without being noticed.

Felix and Uly: Formal Special Forces operatives. Given their size (both are nearly six feet eight inches tall) and matching buzz cuts, they could easily be mistaken for brothers. Their strength, expertise in hand-to-hand combat, and knowledge of nearly every type of weapon imaginable make them invaluable members of Boone's squad.

I, Q: The story so far . . .

Quest (Q) Munoz and Angela Tucker are new stepsiblings. Their parents are the two halves of the musical act, Match. After their parents marry at a ceremony in San Francisco, Q and Angela accompany them on their national tour. They travel the highways and byways of America in a multimillion-dollar coach.

As Q and Angela get to know each other, Q learns Angela's mother was a highly decorated Secret Service agent. Malak Tucker died in the line of duty. She was trying to defuse a bomb set by a terrorist group at Independence Hall in Philadelphia. It's Angela's dream to one day follow in her mother's footsteps and become an agent.

Angela learns that Q lived for years on a sailboat with his mother. His father was another musician, the famous Speed Paulsen. His parents had a contentious divorce and Q and his mother have made their own way together for many years.

Q likes and respects Roger, his new stepfather, and is happy for his mom, Blaze. Q has a casual attitude toward school and homework, and his first love is magic. He wants to be a magician someday and his cargo pants are full of decks of cards, colored scarves, and magic coins.

On their first night out of California, their coach breaks down in the Nevada desert. Q awakens and takes a stroll outside to find an extremely old, very wrinkly, and mysterious man slumbering by their coach in a sleeping bag. He has some camping equipment, a stack of James Bond novels, and perhaps the world's oldest and smelliest dog, Croc, with him. He tells Q his name is Tyrone Boone. But everybody calls him Boone.

As it turns out, Boone is a roadie. A roadie is a jack-of-all-trades in the music business. Usually they work with a group or a performer and do everything from driving the bus and setting up all the equipment for each concert, to fixing broken instruments and generally anything else that needs doing. Boone has been in the music business for a very long time and Blaze Munoz-Tucker has worked with him before.

Q and Angela aren't too sure about Boone. For one thing, he knows a lot about everything. He has incredibly detailed information about the history of every town they pass through. He has knowledge about things that most people wouldn't know. And, as it turns out, Boone is not what he seems.

The bus is being followed. No one knows for certain by whom

or why. But Boone seems to know who is following them. More importantly, he appears to know more about how to get rid of them than a roadie should.

When they arrive in Philadelphia, Angela receives the shock of her life. She learns that her mother, Malak Tucker, is not dead. Angela discovers that her mother had an identical twin sister, Anmar, when they were born in Lebanon. Separated from Malak at birth, Anmar grew up to become one of the most feared terrorists in the world, known as the "Leopard." Angela learns that years earlier Anmar contacted Malak (who was unaware of her existence), explaining she'd had a change of heart and no longer wished to be a terrorist. She told Malak she was on her way to Independence Hall to defuse a bomb that had been planted there. Malak raced there to help her. But she arrived too late and Anmar was killed in the explosion.

Seeing an opportunity to infiltrate a deadly terrorist cell, Malak went undercover, impersonating Anmar. To do so, she gave up everything. Her husband, Roger, and her daughter, Angela, needed to believe she died in the blast. Malak made this sacrifice and has spent the past several years working her way up toward the top of the cell's power structure.

Boone soon determines that a rogue Israeli Mossad agent, Eben Lavi, and a team of assassins are the ones tailing them. Eben holds Anmar (Malak) responsible for the death of his brother. He believes Angela has some information that may lead him to the Leopard.

In Philadelphia, Angela meets her mother in secret. She is overwhelmed at learning her mother is alive; Malak insists Angela and Q must keep her secret. They also discover that Boone is not just a roadie. He is a "NOC" CIA agent. NOC stands for No Official Cover. It means that Boone is working outside official CIA channels. If he is caught or captured, he will have no diplomatic immunity and the government will deny his very existence.

Boone and Malak decide the best way to stop the cell is for her to continue her ruse. Angela and Q are now privy to a deadly secret and when Eben Lavi takes them hostage, Boone must take extraordinary measures to keep them safe.

After Philadelphia, the next stop on the tour is a special concert at the White House. Q and Angela, along with their parents, stay overnight in the White House guest quarters. In the middle of the night they are summoned to the Oval Office by J. R. Culpepper, president of the United States. And they are shocked to find Boone sitting there, chatting with the president. The president praises them for their actions in Philadelphia and gives them special gifts—Omega Seamaster watches that have the president's private phone number engraved on them. Each watch contains a tracking device so he can find them if they are ever in danger. The president tells them they may use the private number any time whenever they need his help and he will take whatever action he can to secure their safety.

As they delve further into uncovering the ghost cell, Q and Angela discover that there is a "mole" in the White House. And they meet P.K., the president's precocious son, Willingham Culpepper. P.K. is ten years old but wise beyond his years. With his help, Q and Angela whittle down the list of suspects. But during the concert in the East Room, they are shocked to discover that the ghost cell has ordered Malak to kidnap P.K. and Bethany Culpepper, the president's daughter. With Malak's help, they foil the kidnapping of P.K. but Malak takes Bethany in order to preserve her cover. She promises President Culpepper she will allow no harm to come to Bethany and will blow her cover to save her if necessary.

In Kitty Hawk, Q, Angela, and Boone, with his team of operatives he calls the SOS team (Some Old Spooks), track Bethany and Malak as they head south from Washington, D.C. But things go sour when the cell makes a switch at a rest stop. Four identical Chevy Tahoes loaded with car bombs appear and they can't be sure which vehicle holds Bethany and Malak. Now they are faced with a terrible decision: save Bethany and Malak or try to take out the car bombs.

In the middle of all of this, to Q's great surprise and consternation, his biological father, Speed Paulsen, appears. He finds Q and inadvertently interferes with his efforts to help Boone foil the kidnappers. When Q and Angela are taken hostage by the cell, the game changes. On a remote island off the coast of North Carolina, Boone must enlist the help of ex-navy SEAL John Masters and a SEAL team to extract Bethany and keep Malak's cover intact.

As the tension rises to nearly unbearable levels, Q and Angela make a startling discovery about Boone and Croc. They have an unusual ability to travel across great distances at incredible speeds. With this capability, they help stage an elaborate ruse to rescue Bethany and preserve Malak's cover. Malak is now on the run with a wounded, high-ranking member of the ghost cell.

With the president's daughter safe, and Q and Angela out of danger, what is their next move? What will happen as Malak climbs to the highest levels of the ghost cell? And does Boone have an agenda of his own?

All of these questions remain unanswered as they head for San Antonio with the SOS crew tracking the one remaining car bomb. And as they get under way, they are shocked to find a very unexpected stowaway hiding aboard the coach.

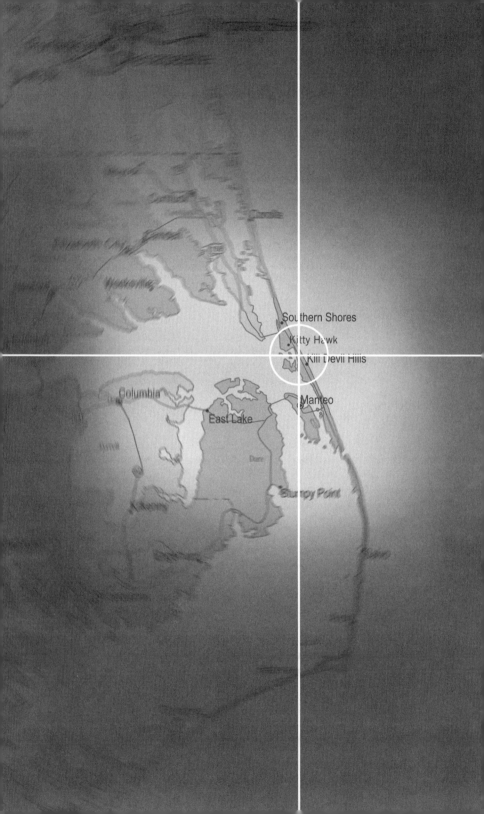

SUNDAY, SEPTEMBER 7 〉

9:16 a.m. to 11:20 a.m.

Speed Bump: "Did somebody say something about breakfast?"

The question made me immediately lose my appetite. It came from my biological father, "Speed" Paulsen, who was certainly not supposed to be in the motor coach. In fact, he wasn't supposed to be in my life at all. Not according to the restraining order. But there he was, grinning, yawning, and strutting out of my parents' bedroom on their million-dollar coach like he owned it. Only Speed could make me forget about food.

Speed is short, with long hair hanging to his shoulders. He always wears cowboy boots with big heels to make him look taller. It never works. His hair was strung with colored feathers. It had glass beads and all other kinds of jewelry and weird stuff braided into it. His jeans were shredded and torn. It would have been a kindness to toss them in the trash. But they probably cost a couple of thousand dollars. He had a big goofy smile on his face as he rubbed the sleep from his eyes.

"Hey, Q," he said. "Where you been, man?"

I was too dumbfounded to answer.

He looked at Angela. "I'm sorry, what was your name again, kiddo?"

"Uh. Angela. And. Uh. Hello," she mumbled. She stared at me in utter amazement. We were certain we'd ditched Speed at a hospital a few miles back up the road. Apparently we were wrong.

Truthfully, it would have been less shocking to see Bigfoot walk out of the bedroom. I was speechless, frozen in place. Boone, on the other hand . . . well, let's just say Boone had a much different response to finding Speed on the coach.

We had just stopped for gas near an outlet mall. Felix, one of the SOS crew, had been driving. He needed to get out to stretch his legs. Boone was a roadie who'd been around the music business for years. He was also a spy. Or had been. Or still was. He was apparently a lot of things Angela and I had yet to figure out.

But right now he was mostly angry. The object of his anger was Speed Paulsen. My biological father, famous rock star, and generally one of the world's most weirdly likeable, yet still thoroughly annoying human beings.

I was standing next to the dining-room table in the middle of the coach. It's where Angela and I spent most of our time. We either did homework or, more likely, used her laptop to keep tabs on an international terror network. Most recently we'd sat there using the laptop to track Bethany Culpepper, the president's kidnapped daughter. Yes. That president. Of the United States.

A few hours earlier, Boone had successfully coordinated Bethany's rescue. She'd been kidnapped by a group of terrorists who called themselves the "ghost cell." Angela's mother, Malak Tucker, was undercover, deep inside the cell. Boone ran the operation that saved Bethany and preserved Malak's identity.

In a night full of strange things, Speed had shown up on the interstate, right in the middle of our pursuit of Bethany's kidnappers. He claimed to be looking for me. According to him, he wanted to spend some time together before he headed to Florida for a vacation. That was a lie. Speed Paulsen rarely paid attention to me. Unless there were cameras present.

Angela had seen Speed in action at a hospital in Virginia a few hours earlier. As I said, we thought for sure we'd successfully evaded him. Wrong.

But now that the shock of seeing him where he wasn't supposed to be had worn off, Boone's anger boiled over. Boone was at the front of the coach. Faster than I could see, he was suddenly behind Speed. It was almost like there were two Boones, like he went through another dimension or some kind of wormhole. Or he hypnotized us. Truthfully, I had no idea how he did it. My life's goal is to be a world famous magician. Boone was performing the greatest magic trick ever right in front of me and I had no clue how he was doing it.

When Boone appeared behind him, Speed yelped. Then he made this really weird *ummph* sound. The next thing we knew, Boone had him on the floor. He was kneeling on top of him, his right knee in the middle of Speed's back.

There was a furious scratching sound at the door of the coach.

Boone glanced up at me. The momentary flash of anger

was replaced by his usual calm expression, as if wrestling a guy half his age was something he did every day. "That's Croc. Let him in."

Speed was trying hard to say something, but all we could hear were grunting noises because his face was buried in the carpet. I cracked opened the door and Croc leaped through it, heading straight for Speed. He crouched near his head, making that low in-the-throat dog growl. The kind that tells you, "make one wrong move and I will bite off your face." Which would have been interesting to see. Croc is possibly the world's oldest living dog and barely has any teeth.

"Get off me, you ancient roadie!" Speed finally managed to twist his head to the side. "And get this dog outta my face, man. His breath smells worse than yours!"

Boone was undeterred. His hands roamed over Speed's back, arms, and legs like he was the star of a TV cop show and had just busted a perp. "Do you have any weapons, Speed?" he asked. "Any needles? Anything sharp that might cut me?"

"What? No, you freakin' geezer! Have you lost what little mind you have left, man?" Speed struggled, but Boone had him firmly on the floor. Boone, laid-back as he was, could occasionally have an edge to him. In the past few days he'd pulled a gun on a Mossad agent. Then he disappeared and reappeared in and around a bunch of heavily armed terrorists like he was in some Hollywood action movie. And they never had a clue he was there. At that moment, Speed was a little overmatched, to say the least.

"Angela," Boone said. "I need you to go outside and keep our driver occupied."

I looked at Angela and she shot me a puzzled glance. Both of us noticed Boone had said "our driver," not "Felix."

Angela's eyes bored into me as she exited the coach. I knew exactly what her look meant. I was going to be quizzed later and I'd better remember every detail. Angela was all about details.

In addition to rescuing people and popping in and out of thin air, Boone was in charge of security for my mom and stepdad's concert tour. Mom and Roger—Angela's dad—had gotten married a few days ago. We were traveling to concert venues around the country. Together they performed as Match. Their newest song, "Rekindled," had rocketed to #1 on the charts and looked like a sure bet to go double platinum. Which probably had a lot to do with the fact that Speed was poking around. If my mom so much as managed to solve the daily *New York Times* crossword puzzle, Speed became insanely jealous. He didn't like it when she succeeded at anything.

Just a few hours earlier, Angela and I had learned about Boone's strange ability. One that Croc seemed to share. It was the kind of stuff we weren't quite able to wrap our minds around. Now we had another thing to add to our ever-growing list. Apparently, Boone was also a grizzled, gray-haired, ponytailed ninja.

Of course, Speed was no threat. The man had the muscle tone of boiled spaghetti and he weighed maybe a hundred forty pounds *if* he was wearing his solid-gold belt buckle that was a replica of the Grammy Award. Which he always was. He never missed a chance to let anyone know he'd won a Grammy. Once.

Boone shifted his weight, holding Speed's wrists in one hand. He ran his free hand along Speed's legs, yanked off his boots, and tossed them in the galley sink.

"Hey, man, those are python skin! They cost more than you make in two years."

"Shut up," Boone muttered. "And you have no idea how much I make."

Python skin. I doubted that. Knowing Speed, they were probably the skin of a velociraptor that had been frozen in ice and that he'd found on the black market somewhere. Speed was about to complain again when Boone quickly flex-cuffed his hands (where in the world had he gotten flex-cuffs?) and lifted him to his feet with one arm. He pushed Speed, not gently, into a seat at the table.

While all of this unfolded before me, I still hadn't moved from my spot.

"Hey, man, what are you—" Speed choked off the words because Croc had jumped onto the table. His snout was now inches from Speed's face. I didn't remember seeing Croc jump up there. Like I said, none of us knew how old Croc and Boone were, exactly. But I knew Croc shouldn't be frolicking around like a puppy.

"What are you doing here, Speed?"

"Screw you, man! Nobody treats Speed Paulsen like this. I'll have you arrested, man."

"Speed. I'm losing whatever patience I had with you, which was miniscule to begin with. What are you doing *here* and how did you get into the coach?" Boone said.

"Up yours, man!" Speed said.

Croc swiveled his head up to look at Boone. They were silent for a moment. I wasn't sure if they weren't communicating via telepathy.

"All right," Boone said. "We'll play it your way." He turned to look at me. "Q, let's step into the rear of the coach. Croc is going to have a little discussion with Mr. Paulsen."

Curiosity killing me, I followed Boone to the back of the tour bus, where Mom and Roger's master bedroom was. I glanced back to see Croc creeping across the table until his snout was less than an inch from Speed's face. He was making that scary growly noise again.

Boone closed the door to the bedroom. A lot of low snarls, unfriendly barks, scratching, and clawing sounds later, we heard from Speed. It had taken less than thirty seconds.

"Come back here, dude, right now! Get this mutt away from me!" he shouted.

Boone inspected his fingernails while I stared at him in disbelief. Finally, I worked up the nerve to speak.

"Uh, Boone?"

"Yeah?"

"What are you doing to my da . . . to Speed?" I was a little torn. Boone had saved our lives. But Speed was still my father. And I'm not the type of person who wants to see anybody get mauled by a mad dog.

"Boone, you freak! Call off this bag of stinky fur, man!" Speed howled.

Boone opened the door and we filed back into the dining area.

"All right, all right!" Speed was pleading now. "Get this

dog away from me, man."

Boone didn't say anything. Croc jumped down off the table and trotted to the shotgun seat of the coach where he sat on his haunches. He stared at Speed as if ready to observe Speed's confession. Or eat him at Boone's command. I wasn't sure which.

"One more time. How did you get into the coach?" Boone asked Speed.

"Q happened to mention there was a hide-a-key in the wheel well," Speed sputtered.

I gulped. He wasn't lying. When we were sitting outside the coach in the yellow Hummer he was driving, I'd told him about the spare key. Now I was worried Boone might be angry, but he didn't seem to care.

"I left the hospital in the Hummer, man. It wouldn't start and some doctor helped me get it running. As soon as I was on the road it acted all funky again and I turned around to go back. I'd lost Q at the hospital but figured he'd show up at the coach eventually. So I got the key and came inside. I just fell asleep in the back is all. . . ." Speed was looking everywhere around the coach except at us.

"Why'd you show up here? Why now?" Boone demanded.

"Why did you drop my Q off on the side of a busy interstate, man? He coulda got seriously hurt," Speed shot back. "I was worried about him, man. Where'd you go to anyway, Q?" he asked me. "I came to the coach thinking I'd check on you. And stuff."

Speed was either using drugs again or rattled by his up-close conversation with Croc. I couldn't be sure. What he was saying was making no sense. And he clearly wasn't fooling Boone. Not for a minute. It also didn't escape my notice that he said *my Q,* not *my son.* Some things never change.

"Your sudden concern is touching," Boone said. "Last time I'll ask what you're doing here. And this time you're going to tell me." Tyrone Boone was tired of Speed's nonsense.

"Okay, okay! I knew the tour was in D.C. I thought I could spend some time with Q before I headed down to the Keys for some R & R with some friends."

That was a bald-faced lie. Not the going-to-the-Keys part, but the spending-time-with-me part. Unless there was a camera or a reporter around, Speed Paulsen had little interest in spending time with anyone except his entourage.

"And you just happened to show up in D.C.?" Boone asked.

"Yeah, man. You know, you hurt my arm," Speed whined.

"Suck it up," Boone said without an ounce of sympathy in his voice.

"Who made you the boss of the world?" Speed snarled at Boone.

"Roger and Blaze put me in charge of tour security." Boone smirked. "You remember them, don't you, Speed? The *talented* musicians?"

Speed drew back as if he'd been smacked in the face. Boone knew right where to apply the needle. Speed Paulsen, *Guitarist* magazine's Guitarist of the Year for eleven years running, was extremely sensitive about his musical ability. He was a fantastic guitar player. That's where he got his nickname. He could pick guitar faster than practically anyone alive. But he wasn't within a dozen counties of my mom or Roger when it came to singing.

"Hey, man—" Speed started to say, but Boone talked right over him.

"Tour security means Q and Angela are in my care. I don't like you, Speed. I've never liked you. Your showing up here, out of nowhere . . . I want to know why."

"I just told you, man. I wanted to see Q," Speed said.

I was going to mention the restraining order. It would have prevented him from seeing me, but thought the better of it. I figured Boone knew what he was doing. Best keep my mouth shut, I decided.

"You and me had our differences back in the day," Speed was saying to Boone. "When I heard you were running security on the tour, I knew you'd keep me from seeing him. Which is totally harsh and unreasonable, by the way, man. So I wanted to get together with him before—" He didn't get a chance to finish.

Hefting Speed up with one hand like he was made of cotton candy, Boone bum-walked him to the small lavatory in between the galley and the master bedroom.

"Hey! What are you doing, man?" Speed protested. "You can't put me in here." His hands were still bound behind him.

"Speed!" Boone said. It wasn't exactly a shout or a threat, but something in the tone made Speed stop squirming.

"You're going to stay in here for as long as I say, until I figure out what to do with you. And you're going to be quiet about it. Or else I'll send Croc in with you. It'll be nice and cozy." He shoved Speed inside and shut the door. There was complete silence from the lav.

Boone strode past me toward the front of the coach. "I need to think," he said. "You and Angela go with Felix to the Big and Tall Shop and also get something to eat. Tell him I'll move the coach after he tops off the tank. Something doesn't make sense here."

Felix needed new clothes because he'd nearly blown himself up when one of the ghost cell car bombs exploded on the side of the road. At the moment, he was six feet seven inches of scorched flesh. He needed duds that didn't smell like smoke in the worst way. I was torn because I thought it might be entertaining watching Felix shop for new clothes. But then, Speed was here and I wanted to know how this was going to play out. Not knowing was going to make Angela grumpy. She'd want to know what he was up to.

"Okay," I said on my way out the door. It was all I could do.

P.K. on the Case:
The White House Solarium

Willingham Culpepper, otherwise known as P.K., the Secret Service code name that stood for President's Kid, fidgeted in his chair. His father, President J. R. Culpepper, was seated to his right, reading through a stack of folders marked "Top Secret" and some files from MI6 marked "Eyes Only." P.K. knew that MI6 stood for Military Intelligence, the British equivalent of the CIA. PK had always gotten a kick out of the Brits and their "Eyes Only" files. How else were you supposed to read a top-secret file? With your butt? He chuckled at the thought of a file labeled "Butt Only." There were also some files from Mossad, Israel's secret service, and a couple of other countries in the stack. He sighed heavily.

"Dad, I just don't want to go to another press conference. Don't get me wrong. I mean, I'm glad Bethany is okay. Really glad. Even though she is a food cop and a homework cop and really bossy about—"

"P.K. . . ." His father had the warning tone in his voice. His dad had been reading the file marked "Top Secret—SOS."

Like, really reading it, as in totally absorbed. Some old roadie named Boone ran the SOS team and his dad had put Boone in charge of saving P.K.'s sister, Bethany. P.K. also knew his dad was smart about these things, having been director of the CIA before his presidency. And this Boone guy and his team *had* rescued Bethany safely.

But P.K. was curious. He knew he'd only been saved from being kidnapped himself by the quick thinking of his new friends, Angela and Quest, and a mysterious woman, Malak Tucker. P.K. wasn't quite sure yet how she was involved, but according to his dad she was a former Secret Service agent who had infiltrated the ghost cell, a super-secret group of terrorists currently at large in the United States.

Chef Cheesy, the White House chef and a member of the ghost cell, had drugged him and tried sneaking him out of the White House. Some of the details were still fuzzy. Angela and Quest and Malak saved him somehow. His dad let Boone go after and rescue Bethany. And he *had* gotten Bethany back safe and sound. But why would his dad send this old guy after his sister instead of sending an FBI tactical team or, well, anybody else. It didn't add up. P.K. hated it when things didn't add up.

In the time it took P.K. to think about all this, his dad had launched into a lecture about how he should respect his sister more. Luckily he was rescued by the arrival of Roger and Blaze Tucker. Two Secret Service agents, Charlie Norton and Pat Callaghan, were trailing along behind them. P.K. knew that his father trusted both men probably more than he trusted the director of the Secret Service himself.

"Roger, Blaze, good morning!" President Culpepper said.

"I hope you slept well."

"Absolutely," Blaze said. "The Lincoln Bedroom is quite nice!"

"I can't thank you enough for your extra efforts on behalf of the bombing victims. I know this has inconvenienced you. But your help means more than you know," the president said. "The kitchen has prepared a buffet, and please help yourself. Bethany will be joining us shortly. She had some last-minute duties to attend to."

In truth, the president had his personal physician up in the White House residence still examining Bethany. They told the doctor she had had a mysterious fainting spell. But she had survived a very close call. President Culpepper was taking no chances. He was having her thoroughly checked out before the press conference.

"Sounds great. We're famished," Roger said, but he didn't sound awfully excited.

"I need to speak to my agents a moment. Please help yourselves to some food and then join us at the table," the president said.

As Blaze and Roger turned their attention to the buffet and the president left the table to speak to Norton and Callaghan, he put the SOS file down on the table. While they were huddled together, P.K. saw his opportunity and took it.

Opening the SOS file, the first thing he saw was a memo, signed by his father when he was director of the CIA. It asked a CIA analyst to investigate the current location of someone named Antonio Beroni. Underneath that page was another old yellowed and wrinkled sheet of paper. Across the top were printed the letters OSS. Because P.K. had been around this stuff his whole life, he knew that OSS stood for Office of Strategic Services–the World War II version of the CIA.

P.K. scanned both memos quickly. His father was still murmuring with the agents across the room. Blaze and Roger were loading up their plates. The older memo said that an OSS operative had successfully been sent through Switzerland into Nazi Germany using an Italian passport. He was now attached to Field Marshal Rommel's staff. His name, according to the file, was Generalissimo Antonio Beroni.

P.K. wanted to read more, but knew better than to press his luck. He had to come up with a reason to get out of the press conference. Roger and Blaze were returning to the table so he quickly shut the file folder.

His mind was zooming a thousand miles a minute. What was a memo from OSS days doing in a file about Boone and his SOS team? And why was his dad, when he was CIA director, asking someone who worked for him to locate an Antonio Beroni? It didn't make sense and things that didn't make sense made P.K. squirm. As Roger and Blaze sat down at the table, it took every ounce of self-control for him to sit still.

Across the room, Agent Norton was keeping P.K. in his peripheral vision as the boy fidgeted in his chair.

"Sir, please tell me you know your ten-year-old son is reading a classified security file?" Norton asked the president.

"I do. But don't worry. It's not Top Secret. P.K. is wound up tight. He doesn't know exactly what's happened here in the last twenty-four hours. So he needs a project. He'll spend some time spinning his wheels on this and then be on to something else. Did you speak to Masters?" the president asked.

"Only when he handed Bethany off to us. He's a good one. Said to tell you, 'We're even,' " Callaghan said.

"I'll never be able to repay him. Did Cheesy or Arbuckle give up anything?" the president asked.

"Not yet. We handed them off to Everett and a couple of other guys Boone called in. They'll hold on to them until this is over. They're close by in case we need them and Cheesy and Arbuckle are also—how should I put this—catching up on their sleep. Figured we'd let them experience what Bethany and P.K. went through. I'm sure they don't know much. It's how these groups operate. I promise you, Cheesy will tell me everything he knows in excruciating detail before I'm done with him," Norton said while grinding his fist in his other hand, the knuckles turning white.

The president shook his head. "Keep Boone's people on them until this is over. No one else but you two are to know where they are. I'll fix it so everyone thinks they came down with the flu or something and they're taking sick days. When this is over they can go to Gitmo for the rest of their lives, for all I care. We need containment on this. But I don't want you leaving the detail here unless I order it specifically. Pat, Charlie, you have to protect my kids," he said. His voice cracked a bit. J. R. Culpepper was not a man who broke easily. But the last few hours had taken their toll.

A look of disappointment flashed across Norton's face. He had looked forward to interrogating Chef Cheesy. Norton was fond of the president's family, especially P.K. The fact that the chef had a role in the attempted kidnapping filled him with rage. But he understood the president's reasons.

"Of course, Mr. President," Norton said.

"Good. Pat, you're here for now. But I'm going to want you to be a floater. Have a grab-and-go bag ready and include your tactical gear. You don't mind taking orders from Boone, do you?" the president asked.

"Sir, Boone is the best agent I've ever seen. And I've been around. If you tell me he's in charge, that's good enough for me," Callaghan answered.

"Good. Now I'm going to go sit down at the table before P.K. uncovers the nuclear launch codes." The president spun on his heel and walked back to the table.

Norton looked at Pat. "You don't think P.K. actually . . ."

Callaghan shrugged. "Wouldn't surprise me."

J.R. reached the table to find Blaze and Roger trying to engage the squirming, toe-tapping, knuckle-cracking P.K. in meaningful conversation. They had plates piled with fruit, yogurt, and nuts and now Roger looked happy. Blaze was picking at her food, looking as if she hoped to uncover a strawberry wrapped in a piece of bacon.

"I don't mean to rush anyone," the president said, "but we have to get to the Rose Garden to get ready for the press conference. Bethany will be joining us there. P.K., you need to change. . . ."

"Dad," P.K. said. "I really don't want to go to this press conference. I've got a lot of homework. In fact, I really need to go to the National Archives for a history—"

"P.K., we've been through this," the president said.

Callaghan coughed from the corner where he had taken

up the usual discreet "Secret Service agent position." "Mr.
President, if I may," he said quietly. The two men stepped out
of earshot.

"Sir, it might not be a bad idea for P.K. to stay away
from the press conference. Purely from a safety standpoint,"
Callaghan said.

"But if the ghost cell doesn't see him . . ." the president
countered.

"They already know they failed getting P.K. out of the
White House. They succeeded with Bethany, but we got her
back. That had to make them burning mad. The fact is, we
still don't know who we can trust. Tell him he needs to go for
the start of the press conference and wave at the camera. Then
we'll take him out of the room. That will be enough to rattle
their cages. Until we know more from an operational security
standpoint, it's better to keep P.K. and Bethany separated.
And if you do suddenly need me elsewhere, keeping him on
the move with Charlie watching him is the best plan."

The president stroked his chin for a moment, then said, "I
like it. Good work."

He returned to the table. "All right, P.K., here's the deal.
You come to the press conference, but only stay through the
opening remarks. After that agents Norton and Callaghan will
take you to the National Archives," he said.

P.K. frowned and crossed his arms, knowing he wasn't
entirely getting his way. At least it was one small victory. He
hated press conferences. Especially when there was more
important work to be done.

Escape

When their speedboat reached the dock across the bay from the breached house, the wounded man—he'd told Malak his name was Paul Smailes or "Number Four"—gave her the keys to a black Chevy Suburban. It was parked in a restaurant near the marina. Malak was able to get him into the vehicle and on the road without being noticed.

As she drove, it became clear his wound was more serious than they had planned. She knew Ziv did not miss his targets, but even he could not control the path of a bullet once it entered the body. Given the rate of blood loss and his rapidly weakening state, Smailes would soon be in shock. She needed to get him to a clinic fast.

"Paul," she said. "Paul! Wake up. We need a doctor. Do you have one nearby?" She kept one eye on the road, one hand on the wheel, and shook him awake. He cried out in pain.

"Mr. Smailes, I need to get you to a doctor," she said. "You must have one somewhere in the area."

By now they had crossed the Morris Harbor Bridge and were heading west on US Route 64.

"Paul!" she said. She had to pay careful attention to her driving. It would be a terrible thing for a police officer to pull them over. But having the man in the seat next to her die would be even more of a problem.

Smailes came awake with a start and another groan. "My . . . phone . . ." he mumbled. With his good arm he pulled a smartphone from his pocket and handed it to Malak. His face was deathly white but he managed to give her instructions.

"Push Star 87. . . . Tell whoever answers your location . . . and you have a package. They'll call back . . . with an address." He barely got the words out before lapsing into unconsciousness again.

Malak took the device, pushed the green "talk" button and the numbers as instructed.

"Cybernetic Research Institute, how may I direct your call?" a voice answered.

"Hello. I am heading west on US 64 at mile marker fourteen. I have a package," Malak said into the speakerphone.

"Thank you. I will call you back within three minutes with the delivery address," the voice said and disconnected the call.

Malak checked her speed and glanced at Smailes. He looked worse. Wherever they wanted her to take him, it had better be close.

In the aftermath of the hurricane, the sky was still slate gray and spitting rain. She looked at the phone and considered calling Ziv with her location. But that was a bad idea. It would leave a trail. Ariel, aka the Lion of God, had given her a phone at the cemetery but using it was out of the question. The cell undoubtedly monitored it and she could not risk making a call. It was also likely the Suburban was wired with audio and video recorders, for in her long journey on their trail she had learned the ghost cell left nothing to chance.

The phone vibrated in her hand and she answered the call.

"This is Cybernetics Research Institute. Thank you for waiting. The directions you require have been downloaded to your phone. Select voice activation on the link and you'll be given turn-by-turn commands." The call was disconnected. Malak pushed the button and a mechanical-sounding voice told her the location was eight miles away.

With her free hand she checked Smailes's pulse. It was faint and his breathing was ragged. She had no time to waste. She hoped he wouldn't die before she could get him treatment.

Malak accelerated, figuring that most of the police and emergency vehicles would be preoccupied with the aftermath of the hurricane. If Smailes died, too many things could go wrong. Not the least of which was the fact that the cell might consider her responsible. Or a loose end that needed to be eliminated. She had very narrowly avoided being exposed in Washington. Only Ziv's quick thinking saved her.

Following the directions given to her by the voice of the navigation application she soon found herself pulling into an industrial park. Maneuvering through the maze of side streets, the GPS indicated they had arrived at their destination. It was a low-slung office building, with two large plate-glass windows next to the front door. There were blinds in the windows and the door was wooden so she could not see inside. A small sign that read "Cybernetic Research Institute" hung above the entrance.

A driveway to the left of the door led to a slatted-metal overhead garage door. As she turned the Suburban into the drive, the door slowly rose. Inside the open space stood a man in medical scrubs.

Malak, the Leopard, slowed the vehicle before pulling into the open space. It was impossible for her to know what might happen next. The man could be a doctor or he could be a "cleaner," waiting to assassinate her and Smailes. Pulling into the garage was a large risk.

With one hand on the steering wheel she reached into the waistband at the small of her back and removed her automatic. With a firm grip on the pistol, she accelerated into the garage. No matter what happened, the Leopard would not go down without a fight.

Speeding Up

Croc sat in the shotgun seat, his eyes following Boone as he paced back and forth. So far there was no sound coming from Speed in the lavatory. Boone had heard enough noise from Speed Paulsen. For the life of him, he couldn't figure out what the neurotic rocker was doing here. The story he'd told about wanting to see Q was a laugh. He'd known Speed and Blaze when they were married and Paulsen was not exactly a caring father.

It was an odd coincidence and Boone was not a man who believed in coincidence.

Croc gave a small bark.

Looking through the coach windshield Boone spotted Angela and Q, followed by the hulking mass of Felix, heading to the outlet stores next to the gas station.

The gas station was a big one and around back had room for trucks and buses to purchase diesel fuel and a large parking area where a couple of semis and a touring coach were parked. Boone fired up the coach and pulled it into the parking area. He found a spot near the rear of the lot and shut off the engine. He pulled his phone from his pocket and punched in a number.

"X-Ray? It's Boone. I need to borrow a tracking device from the coach. Where are they placed? I know you've got backups."

"What's going on?" X-Ray asked.

"I'm not sure. But I need one. Small, something that can stand up to a little jostling," he said.

X-Ray told him where he could find what he was looking for and Boone hung up and fished a screwdriver out of one of the drawers in the galley. Kneeling under the sink, he found the device. It was about the size of two pennies glued together. He pried it loose. Boone marveled at X-Ray's creation. It was amazing to him that he could make something so small, give it an internal power source, and keep it running for days on end.

Speed's boots were in the sink where Boone had tossed them. With the screwdriver he pried the heel off the right one, hollowed out a small spot with the tool, and inserted the device inside it. He tapped the heel back into place. Croc growled his weird growl then barked his approval.

"I know," Boone said, "let's just hope it works."

Boone opened the lavatory door. To Boone's everlasting disgust, Speed was sitting on the toilet, his pants down around his ankles.

"Dude!" Speed said. "How about some privacy, man?"

"Want to tell me how you did that with your hands secured behind your back?" Boone asked.

"I'm skinny, man. When you ain't got hips your pants just

slide right down and . . . and . . . when you gotta go, you gotta go, man."

"You're . . . you . . . Just pull your pants up and get out here," Boone said, backing away from the bathroom door.

"This is harsh, man," Speed said, emerging a few moments later.

"Good." Boone took a multi-tool from his pocket and cut the flex-cuffs. He pushed Speed toward the rosewood dining table and he stumbled into a seat. Boone tossed the boots into Speed's lap. "Get your boots on and get out of here . . . now," Boone said.

"What? You can't be serious, I want to spend . . ." Speed whined.

"Croc!" Boone said. Croc leaped off the shotgun seat, slowly stalking toward Speed, barking and snarling. It was as if the only thought in his canine mind was ripping out his rock-star throat.

"I'm outta here. Call off that mutt, man!" Speed hollered as he slipped on his boots.

"Croc," Boone said. The dog sat back on his haunches, eyeing Speed, ready to pounce at the slightest provocation.

"Okay, man," Speed said. "You can drop me off . . ."

"Get out now," Boone said.

"Dude! Come on! It's pouring down rain out there, man. I can't do rain, man! Drop me off at the next . . ."

"Get out," Boone said.

"Boone, I'm serious, I don't like rain, and besides you've got plenty–"

"Croc!"

"No! No!" Speed shouted. "All right, man, I'm going. Jeez. Harsh, dude."

He pushed past Boone and made his way to the door and opened it, staring at the pouring rain.

"Dude, you got an umbr–"

"Croc!"

Croc launched himself toward the door. Speed jumped and nearly fell to the pavement but recovered and started running. Boone watched Croc chase him across the parking lot toward the interstate. It looked like it was the most fun Croc had experienced in weeks.

Boone called X-Ray. He found it a little spooky that X-Ray always seemed to answer before Boone even heard the phone ringing.

"You got a signal outside the coach?" Boone asked.

"Yeah, it's headed east of your location. Pretty quickly, actually," X-Ray said. "Like something's chasing it. What is it?"

Boone ignored the question. "Good, do whatever you need to do so we can track that signal on Angela's laptop and all of our phones. We're near an outlet mall. Q needs a new phone and you need to clone it so Blaze can call him."

"I texted Felix to send me a photo of the serial number on the box as soon as he buys it. I'll have it powered up and ready in no time."

"Good. Are you still reading the signal outside?"

"Yep, it's about a half-mile from your location now, next to US 64. What are you tracking, Boone?" X-Ray asked.

"I'm not sure," Boone said, disconnecting the call. A few

minutes later, Croc hopped into the coach through the open door. In his mouth was a plastic bag full of the contents of Q's pockets. Croc ran out through the door again and a few seconds later returned with Angela's tattered backpack. A few hours earlier, they had been forced by the terrorists to empty their pockets and leave their stuff behind. After chasing Speed off, Croc must have remembered and hunted it down. Boone was certain that if it were possible, the old dog had a smile on his face.

"Good dog," Boone said.

Shopping for Answers

The rain had eased somewhat, but with the recent horrible weather the outlet mall was nearly deserted. I thought this was a good thing, given the way Felix looked. Essentially he was six-seven and nearly three hundred pounds of scorched skin, leather, and cotton. Even his face was darkened where the explosion had actually abraded his skin, embedding dirt and grit where it wouldn't be scrubbed out for a while. His right eyebrow was singed almost completely off and he was limping, but only slightly. He was also wet, making him smell like something burned, and feeling a little moody.

Angela was giving me all kinds of looks. I could tell she was dying to know what had taken place in the coach with Speed. When I was sure Felix wouldn't notice, I put my finger to my lips and nodded my head toward him. Angela gave me the stink eye again, but finally gave up. She would have to wait until Felix was out of earshot.

We entered the store looking like a couple of drowned rats. A clerk who was Felix's polar opposite met us at the door.

The man stood no more than five-six and had thin wispy gray hair and a stringy mustache. He wore Coke-bottle eyeglasses perched on his nose and couldn't have weighed more than one hundred fifty pounds. He must have been nearsighted because he pounced on Angela and me the minute we walked in. Invading our personal space, he studied us intently, looking us up and down as we dripped water on the store carpet. He hadn't seen Felix holding the door behind us. Yet.

"Can I help you?" he asked. There was an edge to his tone, and he probably thought since we were neither big nor tall we were probably there to shoplift or make trouble of some kind.

"I need new clothes," a voice said.

When Felix stepped through the door from the gloom outside and the clerk could see him clearly, the poor man physically jumped. To say Felix towered over him was an insult to towers. It was like a Great Dane looking down at a Chihuahua.

"Eh . . . hah . . . yes . . . *yessir*," the man stammered. "Your name is Stan. . . . I mean, my name is Stanley. What exactly are you looking for?"

"Everything," Felix said.

"Uh, sure. We can do that. Do you know your size?" Stanley asked. Beads of sweat popped out on his forehead even though it was chilly in the store.

"Five XL," Felix said.

"All right," Stanley said, "let's start with shirts, shall we?"

Stanley led Felix to the back of the store while Angela and I waited near the front.

"Tell me everything," she said as soon as Felix was out of

earshot.

"There's not much to tell. He locked Speed in the bathroom and then he made me leave. As far as I know, he's still in there," I said.

Angela bit her lower lip, which is what she does when she's thinking hard and working her way up to a question she doesn't necessarily want to ask. I had seen her mother, Malak, with the same tic a few hours earlier.

"Q, what do you think Speed was doing there?" Angela asked. "I thought we ditched him."

I shrugged. Angela had a suspicious streak. She likely got it from her mom and it's probably what makes Malak a great agent. You learn to suspect everything when you're in charge of protecting people.

"I don't know. He made up some story about wanting to spend time with me. Which is a total load. My guess is he wanted to find my mom and see if he could spoil her day. That's what he loves to do more than anything."

"Maybe. It's just weird, him showing up out of the blue like that," Angela said.

"I know. Boone said the same thing. But spending time trying to figure out Speed Paulsen is an exercise in humility," I said.

Angela laughed. "I think you mean futility. And you did that on purpose."

"I know." I admit I enjoyed teasing her.

"Boone sure went medieval on him, though," she said. "He doesn't like him, that's for sure."

"Speed Paulsen has to pay people to like him. According

to everyone we've met on this tour, Boone has been a roadie forever. They've probably clashed before. But that's not surprising. My dad has managed to pretty much alienate everyone in the music business except his hired help."

We spotted Felix in the back, shaking his head at a polka dot shirt Stanley was holding up for him. The shirt was roughly the size of a circus tent. I could feel my mind going into acceleration mode and reached into my cargo pants for a deck of cards. I had forgotten that a few hours earlier a now-dead terrorist had made me empty my pockets. My cards, my magic coins, all my stuff was in a plastic bag by the side of the road somewhere several miles back. For a moment, I didn't know what I was going to do. Shuffling my cards and splitting and cutting the deck was how I calmed myself. It annoyed Angela and virtually everyone else, which usually made it that much more enjoyable for me.

Now all I could do was clench and unclench my fists. Angela didn't seem to notice, or if she did, she didn't say anything about it.

"Okay, ever since right before we got nabbed by the terrorists and saw Boone do whatever it is he did, we haven't had a chance to discuss it," Angela said.

"What did we see?" I asked.

Angela punched me in the shoulder. "You know very well what we saw. The traffic jam where he covered all that ground in seconds. And in the coach, just now with your dad, he was up at the front, then he was all the way in the back and I never saw him move."

"Yeah," I said, looking down at my empty hands. I

mimicked fanning a deck of cards open in my right hand. It didn't help. "There's more. At the house Boone popped out of thin air right behind one of the shooters outside. Croc moved like a greyhound on steroids while we stood watch on the overpass. Croc knew Bethany and your mom were in that seafood truck. Just now he jumped up and down on the dining room table like a jackrabbit. And . . ." I stopped. It sounded crazy. And I was starting to get hyped up. I tried to take deep breaths so I wouldn't talk so fast.

"Don't forget the cemetery, and then when we got to the house Croc was already there, across all that water! And what did Boone mean when he said they killed the last vampire one hundred years ago? There's no such thing as vampires."

"Millions of teenage girls would disagree with you," I said with a chuckle.

"Q!" Angela was getting agitated and it was hard to blame her. Her mom was who knew where, doing who knew what. Malak was most likely surrounded by very dangerous people.

"What can I say? He disappears and reappears out of thin air. I've studied magic since I was little. I have no clue how he does it. It's got to be an illusion. The only other possibility is that it's *not* magic, and he can travel through time and space." There. I said it.

Angela is more practical than I am. "How is that possible? It defies the laws of physics and . . . everything," Angela said, looking at me like I was from outer space.

"True. But he did it. In the coach and during the traffic jam. We both saw it and we can't both be hallucinating. And when Croc went after Speed, it looked to me for a second like

Croc got . . . younger. He's old and smelly and sleeps all the time. Then the next thing you know he's bouncing around like an alpha wolf trying to bite Speed's head off or something."

Angela crossed her arms. This was a new posture for her. I fake-shuffled the invisible deck again. Angela pretended not to notice. I was going to have to go to the gas station or somewhere and see if I could find a deck of cards.

"When we get back on the coach we're going to confront him," she said.

"I don't think that's a good idea," I said. "Maybe we should just wait and observe."

"Wait for what? Do you really think Felix and the other SOS members don't know about Boone and his mysterious power? And besides, you had the perfect chance to interrogate him in the coach just now and you didn't. We're wasting time."

"Are you forgetting the Speed-Paulsen-being-there part? What was I supposed to do, ask Boone a bunch of questions and risk Speed hearing? I don't see how this is my fault. I told you I saw him appear right outside the house minutes before the raid. He looked right at me. Knowing me like he does, he realizes I'm not going to keep that to myself. So he knows you're also aware of everything I saw. Besides, he warned us we were going to see him do weird stuff, remember?"

Angela sighed and uncrossed her arms. "I guess you're right. But it's just so frustrating not knowing what's going on."

The difference between me and Angela is that she likes to know every detail of what's happening every single second. I don't mind being left in the dark. It requires less thinking. But right then, a part of me was dying to know how Boone pulled off his magic trick. I closed my eyes and tried to zip away—or whatever it was Boone did. I opened my eyes. No luck. I was still standing in the same place.

"What did you just do?" Angela asked me.

"Nothing," I said.

"You just tried to disappear like Boone, didn't you?"

"No," I lied, because I had so totally tried that very thing. It was amazing that Angela and I were still getting to know each other, but she already knew me so well.

Trying to get her attention off of me, I looked past her toward the rear of the store and the dressing rooms. It worked. She looked over her shoulder to see Stanley, the tiny haberdasher, pacing nervously in front of the dressing rooms. Felix was apparently trying on clothes.

"As I was saying, let's watch and observe," I said. "He's been in the music business a long time. He had to leave a trail. Maybe we can find out more about him on the Internet or something. To me it just doesn't feel like the right time. I say we ask around for more info first."

"And how are we going to get more info?"

I shrugged and did a pretend one-handed cut of the nonexistent deck of cards.

Angela nodded toward the rear of the store, where Felix was coming out of the dressing room in a whole new outfit. He pushed a big pile of burned clothes into Stanley's outstretched hands. The poor clerk looked like someone had handed him a bag of cow manure.

Felix reached back into the dressing room and removed a bunch more shirts and pants before heading toward the register.

As Angela and I followed him, she said, "I think I know who would be a good place to start for some information."

Farther In

Malak helped the doctor move Number Four, now unconscious, on a stretcher from the garage into an examination room. She did not ask his name and he did not give it. The room was fully stocked with medical supplies. But it was certainly not a usual doctor's office. The Leopard marveled again at the ghost cell. She wondered how many facilities it could possibly have like this one, hidden deep within everyday American society, and how many of them went unnoticed.

The doctor worked quickly and efficiently. Once they placed Smailes on the examination table, he had an IV and plasma hooked up and flowing within minutes.

"What happened?" the doctor asked.

"A single gunshot to the shoulder. A .40 caliber, I believe," Malak said. She provided no more detail than was necessary. Using surgical scissors, the doctor cut away the gray sweatshirt Smailes was wearing and uncovered the wound.

"How long ago?" the doctor asked.

"An hour, maybe a little more."

"He's in shock." The doctor maneuvered a portable X-ray machine over Smailes's chest. "Step over here," he said. He guided Malak behind a divider in the room while he snapped the X-rays. There was no need to wait for film. Images appeared on a monitor attached to the wall.

"This is not good," the doctor said.

"What?"

"The bullet must have deflected off the clavicle or rib cage and collapsed his lung. Given the damage, he's going to need more treatment than I can give him here," the doctor said.

"No," Malak said. "You will treat him here. We cannot risk exposing him to a hospital and the questions that will follow."

"I can stabilize him, but I'm not equipped for such delicate surgery. If we come up with a story—"

"No. If you need assistance, you bring others here. He does not leave here until he is well."

The doctor opened his mouth as if to explain again, then seemed to think the better of it. He understood that Malak was highly placed in the cell. She very clearly outranked him. With a sigh he left the divider and hurried to his patient's side. Taking a hypodermic needle from the tray next to the examination table he started filling it from a small vial.

"What are you doing?" she said.

"Inducing a medical coma. If I can slow his heart and respiration rate, perhaps I can get him stable enough until we can get him to a trauma team . . ."

The doctor visibly started when Malak drew her gun and pointed it at him. She needed information from Number Four, so he couldn't remain unconscious.

"No," Malak said. "No coma. In fact, wake him up. We need to talk. I need to discuss an urgent matter with him."

"He's barely holding on. If I give him a stimulant, he could–"

The sound of Malak pulling back the hammer of the automatic with her thumb interrupted the doctor. "Do it," she commanded.

The doctor returned the needle to the tray and picked up another one. His hands shook nervously as he filled it with a clear fluid. He injected it into the IV. Nothing happened for a few minutes, then Number Four came awake suddenly.

"Where am I?" he asked, his voice a grating rasp.

Malak lowered her weapon, but kept it in her hand. "Leave us," she ordered the doctor, who scurried away into the outer room. When she was sure he was out of earshot she turned to the injured man.

"You were wounded. Do you remember?"

"Vaguely. You . . . it was . . . you shot those men. You saved my life."

"None of that matters. The doctor says you are unable to travel. I need to know what I am to do. What are my instructions?"

Smailes closed his eyes and swallowed. "San Antonio. There is a plane arriving shortly at Manteo airport. Take my phone. Press Star 99. The pilot will answer and give instructions. . . ." His voice trailed off.

"Why San Antonio? What do I do when I get there?" Malak raised her voice, trying to cut through the fog shrouding the wounded man.

"You'll meet . . . the rest of the Five . . . is . . . there. The plane . . . take . . . you," he managed and then lapsed back into unconsciousness.

"Wake him up," Malak called out to the doctor in the other room.

The doctor rushed back in, putting his stethoscope on Number Four's chest.

"If I try waking him up again he'll die. He might still die," the doctor said, now clearly worried that his patient might in fact pass away and he would be blamed for it.

Malak returned the pistol to her waistband and tapped her hand on her right thigh while she considered her options. She could not get on the plane without letting Ziv know where she was going. An idea came to her. Removing Smailes's phone from her pocket she watched while the doctor ministered to his patient. It would help with her plan. She pushed the numbers as Smailes had told her to.

A man answered.

"Mr. Smailes gave me this number. He is unable to come to the phone," she said.

"We've been expecting you. We're currently inbound to Manteo airport. There is a private hangar, number 23, at the far west end of the field. We'll be waiting. After the jet is refueled we'll depart." He disconnected.

"Can you . . . hello?" she said. For the doctor's benefit she shook the phone, pretending to press the button again and holding it to her ear.

"The weather must be interfering with the cell service. Do you have a landline?" she asked the doctor.

"In the next room," he said absentmindedly as he worked on Smailes's shoulder.

Malak walked into the next room. The phone was on a wall next to a cabinet full of medical supplies. Taking a deep breath, she paused a moment to think. After years on the trail of the ghost cell, she was closer to destroying it than she had ever been. In the last few hours she'd learned their leadership council amounted to five members. Number Four now lay on a gurney, barely alive. In her experience, the cell watched and seemed to know everything. They were the most cautious and careful terrorists she had ever faced. They had eyes everywhere, countersurveillance and resources such as medical clinics all over the country. The security around their top leadership would be even more impenetrable. From now on, she had to remember that she was likely being watched or at the least listened to in every vehicle, every room, and anywhere she went. The next few hours would be critical, not only to her mission, but to remaining alive. The Leopard would need to stalk her prey more carefully than ever.

Making the call on the clinic phone would require a bit of acting on her part. She pretended to try using the phone one more time, moving it around in the air, and fake-pushing random buttons, letting whomever might be watching know she couldn't get a signal. Shaking her head, she lifted the receiver on the wall phone. Standing very close, her body shielded it so that no camera could see the number she dialed. First she called Ziv.

She was relieved to hear him answer but could do nothing to show it.

"Yes," she said, knowing he would recognize her voice. "My cellphone dropped the call and I did not hear the end of your instructions. Paul Smailes told me we are flying to San Antonio. I heard you say an airfield in Manteo? Then the call disconnected. I am having trouble with cell reception. Yes. Manteo airport, hangar 23. I will be there within the hour. I am driving a black Suburban. Make sure I am expected. I will leave Mr. Smailes's phone on while I'm driving in case you need to reach me." She hung up, letting out a big sigh. Ziv would instantly understand her message.

The Leopard was on the move, she was in danger, and Boone and his team would need to track her flight. His technical mastermind would need to hack into the smartphone to erase the call record. Boone and his crew were top-notch. She hoped they could do everything that needed to be done in time. The plane would be the easiest part. Not even the ghost cell could hide a jet from air traffic control and satellite tracking.

Malak put the phone in her pocket and walked out to the garage without speaking to the doctor. Her sudden disappearance would unsettle him. Number Four was no longer her concern. He was in no shape to do much, even if he recovered. She supposed they might check the number she'd dialed on the landline, but hoped she'd sold the fact that her call dropped, and it would be overlooked.

In the garage she spied the button for the overhead door. She pushed it and the door rose slowly and silently. Climbing into the SUV she started it up, backed out of the building and onto the street.

Inside the temporary safety of the Suburban, she took a deep breath and tried to relax. Focus was required. She recalled her conversation with Boone in the cemetery, a few hours earlier. She had become Number Five. Smailes was Number Four and was gravely wounded.

That left three more for the Leopard to hunt.

Not on My Watch

Eben Lavi felt like someone had punched him in the chest with a concrete fist. Malak Tucker, known in the international terrorism community as the Leopard but in reality a deep-cover Secret Service agent, had shot him during the rescue of Bethany Culpepper. Malak was on the trail of the ghost cell. In order to maintain her cover, they'd choreographed an elaborate plan for her to shoot him in his center mass while the SEAL team rescued the president's daughter.

His ballistic vest had prevented him from being pierced through the heart, but the shot had also catapulted him into a wall and his back was killing him. Their charade had worked to perfection, but the pain was still intense. Eben had not yet worked his way up to deep breaths.

"You look pale," Ziv said. Eben couldn't be sure but he thought there might be a hint of sarcasm in Ziv's tone. With Ziv it was always hard to tell. He was Malak's father. For years he'd protected her while she chased the ghost cell. He referred to himself as "the Monkey that watches the Leopard's tail." It was a classic countersurveillance technique–someone watching you while you watched the target. He'd spent the last few years of his life following her–without her knowledge until only recently–guarding her back and making sure she didn't walk into a trap.

"You are quite a comedian," Eben said, his breath coming in short gasps. "When this is over you should take your act on the road. Preferably a road that leads far, far away from me."

In truth, Eben was starting to grow somewhat fond of the older man. How was this possible? They should be enemies. Eben was one of Mossad's finest agents, or at least he had been once. In Philadelphia he sent his two fellow agents back to the Institute, telling them he'd killed the Leopard, completing their mission. But so far no one had reached out to him. His status might have changed since he had gone off the grid with Boone and his SOS crew. Mossad, Israel's intelligence agency that was similar to the CIA, had been his life. But now he sat next to a former enemy, a man who had once been a terrorist and assassin. The irony did not escape him. It would forever be necessary to guard against those who sought to do harm by violent means. But he now wondered if relationships could change and conflicts be prevented if adversaries took the time to get to know each other. What if they shared common goals? He found himself pondering this very question the more time he spent with Ziv.

Ziv chuckled. "I don't know what you're whining about. I'm nearly twice your age and my own daughter just shot me two times. You don't hear me complaining. I think you should do as the Americans say and 'shuck it up.' "

"That is not what the Americans say." Eben winced. "It's 'suck it up.' "

"Are you sure?" Ziv asked.

"Quite," Eben said.

"That expression makes so much more sense now," Ziv said, taking a sip from his bottle of water.

They were in a nondescript hangar at the far end of the First Flight Airport in Kill Devil Hills, North Carolina. After a helicopter had evacuated them from their elaborately staged raid, navy SEAL John Masters accompanied the president's daughter on her return to Washington aboard a CIA Gulfstream jet. She was likely back in the White House by now.

The two men were quiet for a moment, each mentally replaying the events of the raid. It was a form of internal debriefing every agent did after an operation. Slowly they reimagined each step. First: Eben bursting through the front door. Then Malak shooting him in the chest. Ziv shooting the man she was with, an *unsub* or "unknown subject" in their trade, who had only been identified as a highly placed member of the group who ran the ghost cell, a group calling themselves the Five.

Malak shot Ziv twice. Eben had to admire the older man's toughness. Even with the ballistic vest he wore, his chest and ribs were going to ache for days. Ziv had stepped about a little gingerly in the minutes right after the raid, but now he acted as if he hadn't felt a thing. He was a tough old bird, Eben had to give him that.

"Are you sure you only wounded the man?" Eben asked.

"It would be a tragedy if he were to bleed out before the Leopard could learn more from him."

"The Monkey does not miss. He is wounded enough so that he is not a threat to Malak, but not so much that he should die from it. If she can get him treatment in time."

The sound of another helicopter touching down outside the building diverted their attention. The SEAL team, at the far end of the hangar, gathered up its gear and exited through a side door. A few moments later a man in a dark suit, black sunglasses, red-and-white-striped tie, and with an American flag pinned on his lapel entered the hangar. He was carrying a small red leather box. Eben and Ziv recognized him immediately as a member of the U.S. Secret Service. When he stopped in front of them he stood ramrod straight.

"Mr. Lavi, my name is Agent LeMaire. The president has asked me personally to deliver this to you," he said, handing the box to Eben.

Inside it Eben found a very fancy-looking watch and a folded piece of paper, which contained a note.

Mr. Lavi,

Mere words cannot measure the amount of thanks I owe you for your actions today. This watch, an Omega Seamaster, is a small token of my gratitude. On the back you will find ten digits engraved in the casing. That is my personal phone number, one that I ALWAYS answer. If at some future time you find yourself in need of assistance, no matter

the hour or where you are in the world, call
this number and I will take whatever action I
can to assist you. This is a very exclusive club
you have just joined. But you earned it.
Regards,
J. R. Culpepper
POTUS

"What does it say?" Ziv asked. Eben absentmindedly
handed the note to him as he put the watch on his left wrist.

Ziv scanned the note quickly. "Where is the box for me?"
he asked Agent LeMaire.

"This was the only box I was given," the agent answered.

"Are you sure?" asked Ziv. His voice carried a mixture of
confusion and disappointment.

"Yes, sir," Agent LeMaire said.

"Please extend my thanks to the president," Eben said.
The light coming through the high windows of the hangar
danced and glimmered off the watch's crystal facing.

"I shall. Now if you gentlemen will excuse me, I must
return to Washington immediately." He turned on his heel
and was gone as quickly as he had appeared.

"It is a very nice watch," Eben said, twisting and turning
his wrist to admire it.

"Hmm," Ziv said, standing up, ignoring Eben's gloating.
His phone chirped and he answered, listening for a few
seconds.

"Understood," he said, snapping the phone closed.

"The Leopard is on the move. The Monkey must guard

her tail. Are you able to travel?"

Eben looked at his new timepiece. "I think I can make the time," he said dryly.

Disgusted, Ziv stalked out of the hangar to their waiting car. Eben was admiring his watch. But Ziv was wondering about Malak. His phone still in his hand, he pushed the button that would connect him with Boone.

Back On Line

After Felix got his new clothes at the Big and Tall Shop, we had to pop into an AT&T store so I could get a new iPhone. It was kind of funny because Felix had the same effect on the AT&T guys as he did on Stanley. Even though his clothes were clean, his face was still darkened by the blast and he reeked of smoke and explosives. The clerk couldn't complete the transaction fast enough.

Outside the store, Felix handed me the bag. Taking the phone out of the box, I powered it on. The phone rang almost immediately. I looked at Felix, completely confused.

"Answer it," he said.

I slid the bar on the screen to the right and lifted the phone to my ear.

"Hello?" I said cautiously.

"Q, it's X-Ray. Hey, listen, I need you to go to the settings icon and turn on the wireless network reception. Do you know how to do that?"

"Sure," I said.

"As soon as you do, your phone is going to be cloned to your old one and it will have the same number, your contacts, texts, history, and all that."

"Okay," I said.

"Catch you later," he said and disconnected the call.

I did as X-Ray instructed and the screen on my phone started blipping all over the place. A few seconds later it was back to normal. Felix looked at me and grinned.

"How did they—" I asked him.

"Hey, I just do what X-Ray tells me," Felix said. "He does all the voodoo. Don't ask me how. I'm the one on the team that usually gets blown up. He sits in a comfortable van and pushes buttons," he said. Felix said it all as if it was normal for a guy in a beat-up van a couple hundred miles away to clone a phone in about three seconds. It's not. And since he'd mentioned voodoo, I wanted to ask him if he knew that Boone zipped all over the place at the speed of light and could apparently travel over water without a boat.

"How—what . . . can . . . I . . ." I was no techie like Angela, who stood there looking a little dumbstruck herself.

Felix shrugged. "You got me. I can fieldstrip a MAC-10 machine pistol in under seven seconds and shoot an apple with an M-4 at three hundred yards, but the tech stuff is all up to X-Ray. Guy's a genius with that stuff. Come on. Explosions make me hungry. Let's get some chow."

Felix headed in the direction of the McDonald's, between the gas station and the outlet mall. Roger had forbidden us to eat at fast-food places on tour. Of course this only made us crave it more. There were some perks that came with hanging out with a bunch of old spooks run by a . . . wizard or warlock or whatever Boone was.

It took Angela and me about three steps for every one Felix made, just to keep up. I was still staring in wonder at my new phone when Angela started her interrogation of Felix. The rain was letting up but we were already wet so there wasn't really much to do about it. Felix walked like he wasn't even aware the rain was falling. Now he smelled like a pile of wet gunpowder.

"So, Felix," Angela said. I could tell she was using her nonchalant voice. As it turned out, Angela was pretty good at this whole everyone's-got-a-secret thing and she wanted to be an agent like her mom. Knowing Angela, she'd probably be director of the Secret Service someday.

"How long have you known Boone?" she asked.

Felix shrugged. "Don't know. Ten, maybe twelve years."

"Really!" Angela answered like she had just learned the most interesting fact in the world. "Where did you meet him?"

"You know, I don't really remember. I think my sniper team was on temporary assignment with Delta. We were deployed to rescue some American citizens who were being held hostage. We parachuted into some place I can't tell you, because we weren't supposed to be there. Our team was supposed to meet our guide, as they called him, who would take us to where we needed to go. Boone was NOC for CIA, but I suspect you know that. We got to our rally point and the guide was Boone. It was about twenty miles outside a city where a concert was going on. Being a roadie is kind of a good cover for him. Even in countries that don't like us much, they'll let the rock bands in. Boone's been in a lot of places."

I was trying to keep up with his strides and pay attention to what he was saying. Delta was Delta Force. It was a Special Forces unit in the U.S. Army. I wasn't exactly sure what it did, except go into really bad places and try to rescue people in trouble. Kind of like the army version of the navy SEALS, which we'd just seen in action. Whatever Special Forces group Felix was in, I guessed it involved a lot of explosions and guns.

NOC stood for No Official Cover. It meant that Boone once worked for the CIA but not on an official basis. If he ever got caught or captured someplace he wasn't supposed to be, doing something he wasn't supposed to be doing, he'd get no help from the Agency. He would probably rot in a jail somewhere. But Angela and I had just learned that Boone came equipped with a double serving of "I bet you can't catch me" juice. It seemed pretty unlikely there was a jail anywhere that could hold him.

"You were in a Delta unit?" Angela sounded impressed. "Like Delta Force? The counterterrorism guys? They're awesome!"

"I was *temporarily* assigned to Delta," Felix said, correcting her, "and they're okay."

"I'm confused," Angela said. "What were you in, if you weren't in Delta?"

"I bounced around," Felix said.

We only had a short distance to go before we reached the door of the McDonald's and Angela seemed to sense that once Felix found food, he wasn't going to be doing much more talking.

"So Boone met you on this . . . mission. Was Croc with him?"

"Croc is always with him."

"Do you think that's strange?" she asked.

"What?"

"Croc. I mean everyone says Croc has always been with Boone. Dogs don't live that long. It's just curious is all, don't you think?"

"Never really thought about it. Probably gets new 'Crocs' from the same breeder or something," Felix said.

The McDonald's was close enough for me to smell. And my stomach audibly rumbled. I was concentrating on the food now. My attention wandered as I considered what I was going to order.

"Really, you've known Boone that long, and you've never wondered–" Angela didn't get a chance to finish her question because right behind us a voice made the two of us jump.

"Wondered about what?" Boone said.

Hunting

Once Malak left the garage she took a zigzag route to the airfield, doubling back a few times. When she was certain she wasn't being followed, she drove directly there. As she had suspected, it was quiet.

At the far west end of the field she spied a white Gulfstream in front of a hangar. She maneuvered the SUV to a parking space near the jet and paused for a moment, her hands on the steering wheel. There was a fuel truck just pulling away from the plane. The door opened and a stairway unfolded until it rested on the tarmac.

Malak the Leopard drummed her fingers on her right thigh, trying to calm herself. Taking several deep breaths had little effect. She was closer to bringing the cell down than she had been since she had taken on the Leopard's identity. Now it felt like she was at the point of no return. The truth was, Smailes said the plane would carry her to San Antonio to meet the other members of the Five. But she had no way to verify this. For all she knew the Gulfstream could be carrying her anywhere. Even to her death.

Contacting Ziv again was out of the question. Somewhere out there was one remaining car bomb. Boone would have his hands full looking for it, plus he also had to get Q and Angela to San Antonio.

Every maternal instinct she possessed told her to restart the Suburban and drive away. To find Angela and never let her out of her sight, no matter the cost. She leaned her head on the headrest and closed her eyes. She was getting so close. If she did not get on that plane there was no doubt the cell would fade away for a while. But eventually they would find her and exact their revenge. The only chance to regain her old life was to see this through to the end. Boone, Ziv, Callaghan, and the president were all watching out for her and now Angela was involved. Her daughter's safety was paramount. That was all she truly cared about.

Angela was her little girl. Of course fifteen was not so little anymore and Angela was full of fight and spirit and possessed a fierce intellect. But Malak had left her. Abandoned her. The reasons were worthy ones, but the ache would never go away. Her actions, no matter how well-intentioned, had put her little angel in danger. It ate away at her.

A man dressed in a short-sleeved white shirt and navy blue khakis descended from the plane and stood at the base of the steps. The weather was clearing. The rain and clouds had moved to the northeast. Now the sun was brightening the sky. The man shielded his eyes against the glare, looked at the Suburban, and glanced at his watch. To Malak he looked impatient. Impatient people made her nervous.

She pulled the pistol from her waistband and released the clip, checking the load. Would she be the only passenger on the plane? Might one of the other Five be waiting aboard? Questions flew through her mind. Every step she took from this point forward led her farther down an unknown path. The cell could have someone waiting for her on the plane. Perhaps, after the fiasco of the raid and Number Four's injuries, she was no longer trusted. Malak cleared her mind and willed the persona of the Leopard to take over. She pushed thoughts of Angela and doubts about everything out of her mind. From this point forward she would remain on high alert.

As always, the Leopard would be ready for anything.

Some Old Spooks

Vanessa was driving and Uly was asleep in the passenger's seat. It felt like she'd been driving for days. Her shoulders were cramping and she was hoping like crazy the SUV they were following made a stop soon. They couldn't pull over, switch drivers, and then take off again, because they might lose the target. With X-Ray monitoring the equipment in the intellimobile, only she and Uly could drive.

Vanessa was getting nervous. The Tahoe was a half-mile ahead. They'd been a safe distance behind for quite a while but one of the problems with trailing a single vehicle with another lone vehicle was that eventually you were bound to be noticed.

"We can't keep doing this," Vanessa said.

"Too bad the drone crashed," X-Ray said. He had a tone. It was the "letting Vanessa know he held her responsible for breaking his favorite new toy" tone.

Vanessa rolled her eyes. She looked over at the sleeping Uly. She had never seen anyone who could fall asleep so quickly and easily. But if necessary he could also remain fully awake for hours.

Up ahead she saw the SUV signal for an upcoming exit. This was it. Probably the last chance they had to stay with them before they either ditched the tail or called in the cavalry.

"X, get a tracking device prepared. Uly, wake up."

Uly came instantly awake.

"Get ready," Vanessa said.

"Ready for what?" Uly asked, not sounding at all like someone who had just awakened from a sound sleep.

"I'm going to distract them while you put a tracking device on their SUV," Vanessa said.

"Me? You sure? I'm not exactly unnoticeable," he said. And it was true. Uly was a near carbon copy of Felix in the size department. Maybe an inch shorter, his hair in a buzz cut, but he was nearly three hundred pounds.

"It's either you or X-Ray. We don't let X-Ray out of the van, where he might have to interact with people. X, give him the tracker," Vanessa said.

"Give me a second," X-Ray muttered. She could hear him opening the tiny drawers on his console and making noise with the tools he kept on his workstation.

"We don't have a second," Vanessa said. The SUV had turned right at the top of the exit ramp and was pulling into a Speedway station.

"Got it," X-Ray said. He leaned forward, handing Uly a small U-shaped piece of metal roughly the size of a quarter.

Uly looked at the bug with a neutral expression. "Uh, X?" he asked.

"Yeah?"

"What do I do with this?" Uly said.

"You'll have to get underneath the rear bumper. This model Tahoe has a steel bar on the frame that attaches to the bumper. Snap the open end of the tracker over the bar and push it flush against the bumper. It's clipped to the rod that way. It's also magnetic. There's a little wire lead on it that will use the metal of the frame like an antenna. It won't accidentally fall off and the signal will be strong enough for us to drop back out of sight. The battery only has about twenty or so hours of juice, though. If they don't get where they're going by then and we can't get air support or more vehicles, we're going to have to get eyes on them some other way," X-Ray said.

"Okay, Uly, be ready," Vanessa said. "The gas tank is on your side. You start filling up the van. They won't leave the Tahoe completely unattended. I'm betting the women will go in together, but at least one of the men will stay with the vehicle at all times. But he's also going to need to use the john, so when the first guy comes back and the second guy goes inside . . . well, you'll know what to do."

The white SUV was parked at an island of pumps and Vanessa maneuvered the intellimobile so the gas cap was facing the SUV on the other side of the island. She shut off the ignition. Just as she had predicted, one of the suspects was filling the tank. The two women and the other man had just entered the station through the glass door. It was a statistically safe bet the women would be inside longer than the man.

Uly got out, stretched and yawned, seeming to pay no

attention to the guy pumping gas. He rotated his neck a few times like a man glad to be free of the monotony of a long drive. When he was satisfied he'd put on a good enough show, he stepped to the rear of the intellimobile and started filling the tank.

Vanessa held her phone to her ear as if she was involved in a long conversation. When the SUV was full, the man removed the nozzle and nested it back on the pump. Replacing the gas cap, he walked to the front of the SUV and put one leg up on the bumper, waiting for his colleagues to return. A few seconds later, his male companion came out of the station with a large cup of coffee. There was no sign of the two women yet. With his companion in sight he ambled toward the convenience store.

Vanessa stepped out of the intellimobile, still pretend-chatting on her phone.

"No, sis, like I said before I left, Boopsie will only eat her Purina. If you give her table scraps you're going to have a really sick cat. . . ." She walked with her head down, as if she were concentrating on her conversation, and bumped into the suspect with the coffee. Even with the lid on, it splashed on his hand and he yelped in pain.

"Gotta go, sis." She snapped the phone shut.

"Sir, I am so sorry. This is totally my fault." Vanessa was perfectly positioned at the front of the van on the driver's side so that Uly was shielded from the man's view.

"Are you okay? Did you get burned?" Vanessa asked him.

After checking the station through the window and seeing no sign of the other driver, Uly dropped to the ground and went under the SUV. His eyes were drawn to something he'd never seen on an automobile before, and he knew his way around a car. It was a stainless steel box welded to the frame adjacent to the gas tank. Blue and green wires ran out one end of it and disappeared through the underside of the Tahoe's cargo area. For the two seconds it took Uly to process all of this, he thought of attempting to disarm it. But there was no time. He had the tracking device in place in an instant and was back on his feet and holding the nozzle. A gymnast would have marveled at his agility.

"Watch where you're going," the guy snapped, shaking his hand.

"I'm really sorry, I have a first-aid kit. . . ." Vanessa stammered, looking like a distressed little grandmother. The fact that she was probably the world's deadliest distressed little grandmother notwithstanding.

The second terrorist approached the SUV with his own cup of coffee and a bag of chips, studying the scene in front of him. Uly frowned at the fact that he looked like a frat boy, not some lowlife ready to blow up hundreds, maybe thousands, of innocent people. All the same, he moved his hand inside his jacket and rested it on the butt of a silenced Heckler & Koch .32 pistol he kept there in a special pocket sewn to the inside of his leather jacket. In his mind he picked his primary and secondary targets. He would shoot the second guy first. Vanessa was close enough to the first guy to take him out if they tried anything. Uly tensed, ready to go cowboy if the situation demanded it.

"What's going on?" the second guy asked.

"It's nothing. Ma'am, I'm sorry I snapped. I was just startled by the hot coffee is all," the first terrorist said. "I'll wash up in the restroom. It's no problem."

"I'm really sorry," Vanessa said to both of them. "My cat gets sick and my sister gives her the wrong food and I–"

"No harm done," the second guy said, opening the door to the SUV and climbing in. Vanessa shuffled into the convenience store and passed the two women coming out. A few minutes later the first terrorist emerged, wiping his hands on a paper towel. He got in and they roared out of the parking lot, turning onto the road leading to the interstate.

"You see anything?" Vanessa asked, when she returned.

"Not inside. Windows in the rear doors are tinted. But there was a box welded next to the gas tank, wired to the interior. It's a bomb," Uly said.

When the Tahoe had turned onto the expressway the side door of the intellimobile slid open and X-Ray poked his head out.

"Is your device working?" Vanessa asked.

"Loud and clear," X-Ray said.

"Good," Vanessa said. "The fact that they're so polite makes me . . . jumpy. They must know they're carrying a bomb and they don't even seem nervous about it." She pulled her phone from her pocket and pushed a button.

"Who are you calling?" Uly asked.

"Boone. He's got some choices to make. A part of me was hoping this might just be a decoy, from the switch at the rest area. But now we know for certain it's a weapon. They normally don't drive one of these vehicles for this long. Too many things can go wrong. The cell isn't normally a bunch of suicide bombers. They pick a target, park their car bombs, detonate them, and move on. Live to bomb another day. Maybe they're changing the game. There is all kinds of crazy going on here. Boone needs to decide if we continue to follow them . . . or take them out."

Quicker Than the Eye

Angela and I jumped at Boone's sudden appearance outside of McDonald's. Felix didn't notice, or if he did, he didn't show it. It was becoming more clear to me that I wasn't cut out for this spy stuff. So far I had had a knife held to my neck, had to escape from a deranged chef, had run through a hurricane to spy on cars, spent way too much time with a smelly dog, been right in the middle of a navy SEAL op, and then there was the pigeon poop I'd gotten all over my hands in Philadelphia. And even worse, I didn't have a deck of cards to calm myself down with.

My nerves were jangled. I needed food and sleep. And my stuff. Not having my stuff was making my mind race to previously unrecorded levels.

"Wondered about what?" Boone repeated Angela's question to Felix.

We were at the door of the McDonald's and Felix was nonplussed by Boone's sudden appearance. Apparently he hadn't heard or didn't care about Angela's questions and headed inside. When he opened the door the smell was nearly overwhelming and my mouth made involuntary chewing motions.

"Where's Croc?" Angela asked, using the old technique of answering a question with a question.

"Guarding the coach. And getting a little exercise. Wondered about what?" Boone was insistent. Smart as Angela is, I doubted she could trick someone like Boone into answering a question. He'd been doing this too long and was too smart to be caught off guard. And also, I doubted Croc was guarding the coach. Sleeping in the coach was a more likely possibility. Smelling up the coach was a certainty.

"We were just talking about Felix and his background. Did you know he was assigned to Delta Force?" Angela said. *Give it up, sis,* I thought to myself. Of course Boone knew this. Felix wouldn't be with SOS if Boone didn't know every detail about him.

"He bounced around," Boone said. "What was it you were wondering about?"

"Actually it was Croc. How everyone says he looks like the same Croc you've always—"

"Good genes," Boone said quickly as he followed Felix into the McDonald's.

"He's really starting to tick me off," said Angela, biting on her lip so hard I thought it would start bleeding. Which meant she was ready to give him a long lecture about keeping secrets from her or something but she was literally biting back the words.

"So much for my idea of getting any actionable intelligence

out of Felix," I said. "He's worked with Boone. He must have seen him do some weird stuff. Or maybe not. Maybe they haven't faced anything like the ghost cell before."

Angela stared at me with an odd expression on her face.

"What?"

"You said 'actionable intelligence,' " she said.

"So?"

"Somebody likes this spy stuff," she said, grinning at me.

"Hah. No thanks. It's hard not to pick up the lingo when you're traveling with a bunch of ex-spooks. Or current spooks. Or whatever they are. But I'll stick to magic. And now," I said, waggling my hands like a magician, "behind this door, I shall make food appear." I held open the door. I could see Angela trying not to fall victim to the overwhelming smells of fast-food goodness. But she still found the energy to roll her eyes at my lame joke.

Just as we were about to head inside, my new phone chirped. It was a text from P.K.

> Thought you might like to see this info on WH renovation. For your project.

There was a link attached. I clicked on it and a black-and-white photo of a man in some kind of military uniform appeared. He was standing in a forest clearing and even though the photo was old and a little blurry and his hair wasn't long or as gray, it sure looked like Boone. Even more, the dog sitting on the ground next to him looked exactly like Croc. That sealed the deal.

"Wow," I said. I handed the phone to Angela and her eyes got as big as dinner plates.

"What is Boone doing in a Nazi uniform?" she said.

"I . . . have no idea. Could–do you think . . ." I was stumbling around for words.

"Do I think what?" she said.

"I mean, I thought he was joking when he mentioned killing the last of the vampires one hundred years ago. But do you think what he does is like some sort of time travel?"

Usually Angela would have rolled her eyes or shot me down for saying something so outrageous. But this time she didn't have a comeback. The photo wasn't lying.

"Tell P.K. we need a source for our assignment. He can send another link. Photos can be faked," she said.

It was my turn to give her one of the looks she usually gave me.

"Angela, after what we've seen Boone do, do you really think the photograph is fake?"

"Honestly, Q, I don't know what I think anymore." She handed the phone back to me. "Just ask P.K. if he can find out if this photo is legit."

After I sent the text, we followed Boone and Felix to the counter and minutes later we were back in the coach. Felix wolfed down three breakfast sandwiches in about five seconds and got behind the wheel. We pulled out onto US 64, heading west, when Boone's phone rang. He listened a minute. "Got it," he said and hung up.

He placed another call. "X? Ziv just called. Malak is flying out of Manteo airport on a Gulfstream. Follow it wherever it goes. She told him San Antonio." He paused, then said, "Good. That's great work."

"They managed to get a tracker on the remaining SUV," he told us. "Ziv heard from Malak. At least we know where she's headed. And no matter what resources they have, they're not going to be able to hide a plane in midair. So we can track her," he said. "The intellimobile is following the last Tahoe. It's wired with a bomb like the others. It's on the interstate, heading west. They're going to keep following it unless it looks like they plan to blow something up. If they do, Uly and Vanessa will take them out. The cell doesn't normally act like this. Something has changed. Why would they keep that SUV on the road this long?"

Boone was pacing and asking questions. So far, the cell had put car bombs in places where they could cause damage. Felix had blown one up. Ziv and Eben had taken out the other. But now this third one was doing . . . what? Boone's face was wrinkled under normal circumstances. Now he was thinking so hard his wrinkles had wrinkles. I could tell the idea of leaving the SUV on the loose bothered him. But he also wanted to know where it was going.

"Boone, what about—" I began, but he held up his hand as he punched a button on the phone.

"Ziv, it's Boone. You and Eben get to Norfolk right away. I'll get a navy jet to get you and your gear to San Antonio. X-Ray will let you know where she lands and you can pick up Malak's tail. Yes. I know about the watches. Yes, I have one.

No, I can't get you one. That's up to J.R. Time to go," he said and hung up, his face somewhat calmer looking.

Boone was going to let the intellimobile keep tracking the Tahoe. Heck, if he had to, he could probably call up J.R. and order an air strike. And then–*poof*–no more Tahoe. But Boone didn't want just to stop four terrorists. He was trying to bring them all down. Besides, an air strike would be hard to keep out of the papers.

Boone was pacing again. He punched another button on his cell phone. "It's me," he said. "I need you to do something." He headed to the back of the coach, near the door to the master suite, where it was hard to hear him. After a few moments of talking he disconnected and returned to the table.

Boone looked at me. "You were saying?"

"Um . . ." I nodded my head toward Felix. "Does he know?" I asked quietly.

"Yeah. I told him about Speed in the McDonald's," he said.

I nodded my head toward the lavatory.

"What about my dad?" I asked. "When do you plan on letting him out? Because . . . well . . . I have to pee."

Boone reached for Angela's laptop. "May I?" he asked her. She pushed it toward him. He clicked on something then turned it around. A map appeared on her screen, showing our location as a green dot moving along US 64. A few miles back was a red dot, taking another highway south.

"I already let him out," he said in a low voice, "about ten miles ago."

It's Complicated

I didn't know what to say. The coach rolled on for about an hour while I kind of stared blankly at the screen showing the red dot slowly moving south. Maybe Speed hadn't been lying. Perhaps he was going to head to the Florida Keys for some R & R after all. I mean, I didn't believe any of Speed's bull about wanting to spend time with me, but I wasn't sure how I felt about Boone just dumping him like that either. But I also wasn't happy with Speed inserting himself into my life whenever he felt like it.

Croc stared at me from the shotgun seat. I always found his one blue and one brown eye a little unnerving. All of a sudden he jumped off his perch and picked up something from the floor with his mouth.

It was the plastic bag full of my cards, ropes, and magic stuff the terrorist had made me empty out of my pockets. Croc walked over and dropped it at my feet. The good news was I had my stuff back. The bad news was the bag was covered with icky dog drool. I gingerly opened it and dumped the contents on the table. Even before I reloaded my pockets, I took a deck of cards and shuffled it several times. It made me feel better.

Croc made another trip to the front of the coach, retrieved Angela's battered backpack, and took it to her. She was also delighted to get her stuff back, but used a couple of paper towels from the galley to remove Croc's slobber from the fabric.

"Listen, Q–" Boone said, but the chirp of my new phone interrupted him.

The caller ID showed Blaze Munoz. For a second, I froze. We'd been out of touch for a while and she was probably going to have a lot of questions. I was a horrible liar.

"It's my mom," I said with a gulp.

"Put it on speaker," Boone said.

"Hi, Mom!" I said extra cheerfully. "You're on speaker. I'm riding shotgun while Boone drives." Which wasn't true, but she didn't need to know about Felix and his still-smelly self who was actually doing the driving.

"Hi, hon! It's so good to hear your voice. Hi, Boone!" she said.

"Howdy, Blaze," he said. "How y'all doin'?" The good-old-boy drawl was back.

"We're good. Where are you?"

"We're heading west on US 64, close to Raleigh. Gonna hook up with the interstate and head to San Antone."

"That's nice to hear, but you want to hear something really cool?" Mom asked.

"What's that?" I asked.

"You'll never guess where I'm calling from!"

"Okay, I'll never guess," I said. "Where are you calling from?"

"Air Force One!" Mom said. For a moment I thought she sounded a little bit like a squealing teenager.

"Really?" I was instantly curious. "Why are you taking Air Force One to San Antonio?" Right then Angela's cell phone rang. I heard her say, "Hi, Dad."

"The president asked us to make some appearances on our way to San Antonio," Mom told me. "Apparently the benefit we did in D.C. raised a ton of money. He wants us to be honorary cochairs of the relief effort. And because he didn't want to mess up our concert schedule, he's flying us to San Antonio on Air Force One!" Mom sounded a little breathless. I heard Angela say "Amazing" in the background and assumed she was getting the same news.

"That's cool!" I said. I'd watched a documentary about Air Force One on TV and it was a pretty remarkable plane.

"And the best part is you and Angela are coming with us! He said we could do the first appearance in Raleigh and pick you guys up. Won't that be—wait, I wonder how he knew you were in Raleigh?" she asked.

"He's the president," I said. "I suppose he knows stuff. He probably just kept track of our progress because he asked you to stay behind and he didn't want you to worry about us." Boone gave me a thumbs-up. I almost convinced myself with that lie.

"I suppose," Mom said. I knew that tone she was using. It was when she was firing up the Momdar—Mom radar—that

I was convinced every mother possessed. Both of us being so close to Raleigh was a big coincidence, and after years of being married to Speed Paulsen she was naturally suspicious.

Angela was finishing her conversation with her dad.

"Anyway," Mom went on, "we're in the air. Marie and Art said you and Angela would meet us on the plane right after we finish the appearance at a Raleigh TV station. We have a few more stops on the way to San Antonio. We get to stay on board overnight and everything. On Air Force One! I have to tell you, Q, it's awesome!"

"I'll bet!" I said. In truth, it did sound pretty cool. But there was something fishy in all this. It smelled like a Boone-fish. For whatever reason, he wanted us out of his hair for a while. I was willing to bet my last magic coin he'd set the whole thing up.

"I can't wait to see you, Mom," I said.

"Me too you, honey," she said. "And I'm sorry I have to go now. Roger and I are rehearsing a public service announcement that's going to play on MTV and some other networks, requesting donations for the victims."

"Okay, see you soon, Mom," I said.

"I love you, Q."

"I love you, Mom," I answered and disconnected the call. Angela hung up a few seconds later.

We both looked at Boone.

"Busted," he said. "Yes. I called J.R. and set it all up. The press conference with Bethany has taken place. The cell now knows they failed. But something has changed. Ordinarily they'd drop off the grid now and live to fight another day. But they've brought Malak into the inner circle. The last thing she was told before the raid was that she was going to Texas to meet the other leaders. We have to follow that trail wherever it leads. I need time and freedom to check a few things out. You two need to be safe. There is no safer way to get you to San Antonio than on Air Force One."

"How do you know what she was told in the house?" Angela asked.

"I was in . . . let's just say I could overhear them talking," he said.

Angela sighed in frustration and still looked unhappy but I could see Boone's point.

"What kinds of things are you going to be checking out?" she asked.

Boone shrugged. "Just things."

"Boone, you promised in Philadelphia that you'd keep us in the loop." I knew she wasn't really mad at Boone and so did he. Angela was worried about her mother and right now she was just a little exasperated.

"I'm not keeping anything from you, Angela. I'm not sure exactly what I'm dealing with now. When I know something, I'll tell you. But I am keeping you safe, like I promised your mother and Blaze and Roger. I don't take that lightly. Plus, I'm saving you about twenty hours on the coach. I'll find out what's going on with your mother, Angela. Understand something. J.R. has given me a lot of latitude here. If I think she's in a situation she can't handle—which is unlikely because Malak Tucker is the best agent I've ever seen—I'll pull her out. You have my word."

It didn't seem to make Angela completely happy, but I could tell it did make her feel a little better.

And if there was a silver lining in all of this, it was this: I was going to get to ride on Air Force One.

Number Three

There was no one else on the plane except the two pilots. One of them told her to make herself comfortable and enjoy the flight. This Gulfstream was equipped with a cabin door. The pilot and copilot shut themselves in and Malak relaxed a little when she heard the lock click into place.

She was exhausted, mentally and physically. The need for sleep would eventually cloud her judgment and dull her reflexes. The Leopard did not take risks, however. She wrapped one end of her belt around the cockpit door handle and affixed the other to a nearby hook in the galley. If the pilots meant her harm, they wouldn't be able to get out without her hearing them.

This plane was smaller than some of the Gulfstream models she'd traveled on before. There were two leather chairs facing each other across a shiny wooden table and a long leather bench along the starboard side of the aircraft. Once she had secured the pilots in the cockpit, she quickly searched the cabin. It only took a few minutes and she found nothing suspicious, like audio- or video-recording devices. If someone eventually confronted her with video of her actions, she would shrug it off. As always, she would simply tell them the Leopard takes no chances.

Looking at the cockpit door she chuckled softly, wondering if the pilots would need to use the bathroom adjacent to the galley. Too bad. They were locked in. They would just have to hold it. She sat back in the seat and closed her eyes.

When the plane's landing gear bumped her awake, she hurried forward, removed her belt from the door, and quickly put it back on. Taking her seat, she looked out the window as the jet taxied to a stop. She checked her watch. The flight had taken a little under three hours.

The landing strip was in the middle of a big ranch. She saw fences and cattle in the distance. Next to the runway was a small building. A four-wheel ATV with a canvas roof attached pulled up with a man at the wheel. Apparently her journey was not yet over. A few yards away, a black Lincoln Town Car sat parked next to the small building.

The pilot emerged from the cockpit, opened the door, and let the stairs unfold until they bumped gently on the concrete. He said nothing as Malak passed by him to the aircraft door. As with most of her encounters with cell members, the less said among them the better.

Once on the ground, Malak took several deep breaths and strode confidently to the ATV. Wearing the sunglasses she kept in her blazer pocket, it appeared that she was facing the driver but Malak's eyes darted everywhere, gathering as much intelligence as she could. It was a technique every Secret

Service agent learned early in training and the reason most of them wore dark glasses when they were on a protection detail. The darkened lenses hid the true target of an agent's gaze.

She climbed into the ATV as the pilots descended the aircraft steps and entered the waiting car. The car followed an asphalt drive leading toward the mansion. Eventually Malak spied it pulling onto the road in front of the property and speeding away.

The mansion rose in the distance, at least a half-mile from the runway. It was a sprawling structure with flat, tiled roofs. Long wings spreading off in several directions gave it a slapdash appearance. Malak took mental note of everything she could see. This isolated location made an ideal hiding place for terrorists.

"We've been expecting you," the driver said. He was big, wearing a black polo shirt stretched tight over a huge chest and bulging arm muscles. His pants were also black and he wore a straw cowboy hat. The heat was starting to rise and Malak felt perspiration forming on her forehead but he didn't seem to be sweating at all.

The ATV turned around and sped down the same drive the Town Car had taken moments before. It took less than a minute to reach the back of the mansion. The driver got out of the ATV.

"This way," he said.

Malak followed him across a stone patio and through french doors. The house was a maze of rooms and hallways, but eventually he led her into a large library. Each wall was essentially floor-to-ceiling bookcases.

At the far side of the room sat a good-sized executive desk, covered with file folders and papers. A finger of smoke curled up from an ashtray, the remnant of a hastily stubbed-out cigarette. Someone had just been in the room.

Pacing slowly back and forth, Malak kept her hands crossed behind her back, certain she was being observed. She studied the room, memorizing as much detail as she could but at the same time trying to appear relaxed. The Leopard did not like being caged.

The door opened and a tall woman with bleached blond hair piled high on her head entered the room. A pair of reading glasses hung on a lanyard around her neck. The woman was heavily made up, and as she walked toward Malak with her hand out, a watch peeked out from under the sleeve of her blouse. It was surrounded by some of the biggest rubies Malak had ever seen.

"Hello, sugar," the woman said, pumping Malak's hand. "My name is Ruby Spencer. Or Miss Ruby to almost everyone.

"But you can call me Number Three."

Air Force One

When we arrived at the airport in Raleigh, we pulled up to a secure area away from the regular terminals. There were a half-dozen armed guards behind a high chain-link fence. Marie and Art were waiting outside it. They were posing as our parents' PAs, or personal assistants. In reality they worked for Boone and were essentially serving as bodyguards. A few hundred yards beyond the fence sat the president's plane.

It's an impressive sight, even from a distance. It's a big plane. The nose is solid blue and the words "United States of America" are painted on the sides. For some reason each letter looks about ten feet tall. The American flag is displayed on the tail and the presidential seal is on the fuselage near the wing.

Boone had said goodbye to us outside the coach. Felix was getting on a plane to San Antonio. He would have a couple of "guys he knew," as he told us, drive the coach the rest of the way. Everything was moving quickly and Boone's goal was to have as many assets on the ground in San Antonio as soon as he could.

"How are you getting there?" I asked Boone. There was no way to tell for certain because she was wearing sunglasses again, but I'm convinced Angela rolled her eyes. We knew how Boone was going to get there. An unusually fast way.

"I'll see you in San Antonio," was all Boone said. He climbed back into the coach and we watched as it pulled away.

"Great," Angela said with a sigh. I tried to think of something I could say to cheer her up but nothing at all came to mind.

We entered the secure area and were greeted by Art and Marie. A Secret Service agent asked us to empty our pockets into big plastic tubs. Another agent went through Angela's backpack. Two more Secret Service agents met us at the steps to the plane, patted us down, and waved a portable metal-detecting wand over both of us.

The next step was a Transportation Security Administration officer with a German shepherd on a leash. They climbed out of an SUV parked near the plane and the dog gave us . . . let's just say, a *thorough* inspection. I was glad Felix hadn't made me hold his clothes with blown-up Tahoe all over them back at the Big and Tall store. Something in the German shepherd's eyes made me think he wouldn't appreciate that very much.

"Nice doggie," I said. Art and Marie and the TSA agent laughed.

After that, we were cleared and Marie and Art led us up the stairs.

The documentary I'd seen didn't do the plane justice. For one, it was probably the cleanest airplane I'd ever been on. Usually when you get on a commercial airliner the entire interior just looks worn and faded. On the president's plane everything gleamed. The carpet didn't have a speck of dirt that I could see. The cabin walls and even the ceiling seemed to sparkle.

Marie and Art led us to the guest area in the middle of the plane just past the wings. There we were introduced to Chief Steward Rogers. He was in charge of the staff on board the plane. His uniform was black with a coat and pants that made it look a little like a tuxedo except for the gold stripes on the coat sleeves.

"It's a pleasure to have you on board, Mr. Munoz and Ms. Tucker," he said, shaking our hands.

"You can call me Q," I said.

"And I'm just Angela," she said.

"Well, I've had the great fortune to meet your parents already. Such nice people and so wonderful of them to be donating their time and talent to such a worthy and noble cause," he said. Mentioning donations made me think of Buddy T., Mom and Roger's pugnacious, irritating, and overbearing manager.

"Did Buddy T. come with Mom and Roger?" I asked Marie.

"Nope." She smiled from ear to ear. "The president said it was a space issue and Buddy had to fly to San Antonio commercial. He refused, so Heather Hughes flew down with him on her corporate jet. They'll both be there when we arrive."

"Poor Heather," I said absentmindedly, which made

Marie laugh out loud. I wish I'd been there to see it when Buddy T. got that news.

"Would you like a tour of the aircraft?" Chief Steward Rogers asked.

"Absolutely," I said.

We took the tour. It's an unbelievable airplane. Chief Steward Rogers explained that, technically, we weren't aboard Air Force One, because the president wasn't with us. The call sign "one" was assigned by air traffic controllers to any military aircraft the president flew on. So the U.S. Marine helicopter he usually took to the White House from Andrews Air Force Base or Camp David outside Washington was Marine One. If he were to fly on a navy aircraft, it instantly became Navy One, and so on. But so many people had come to refer to the actual plane we stood on as Air Force One that the name stuck.

The plane was a specially converted Boeing 747. It had four thousand square feet of space on three different levels. We weren't allowed everywhere, but we learned a lot of cool stuff. The communication systems allow the president to speak with anyone anywhere in the world. The wires and components are specially shielded from the electromagnetic pulses caused by nuclear explosions, so they wouldn't go offline in the event of an attack. Unlike a civilian airliner, Air Force One could also launch countermeasures, which were super-hot flares the plane ejected to draw away heat-seeking missiles. Like I said, pretty awesome.

When we returned to the guest area, Chief Steward Rogers asked me if we would like anything to eat. My stomach growled even though we had eaten just a couple of hours earlier.

I glanced at Marie and Art. "What time will Mom and Roger be back from their appearance?"

"Not for another hour or so," Marie said. Apparently Art was not the talkative type. He was pleasant enough, though. Hearing about Felix being in Delta Force had made me question the background of all of the SOS groups. Art always seemed to be "on duty," which was probably an ideal quality in a personal assistant/bodyguard/spy/likely ninja assassin.

"Could I get a cheeseburger, fries, and a vanilla milkshake?" I asked Chief Steward Rogers.

"Of course!" he said, beaming. "And for you, Ms. Tucker?"

"I'll just have some green tea," she said. *Party animal*, I thought to myself.

"Right away," he said and disappeared.

I plopped down across from Angela. She was slouched in her seat, the tray out, and her laptop flipped open. Angela was tethered to her laptop. I had one just like it and hardly used it. Luckily she was hyperorganized and had been doing a ton of work for our school project. I was way lucky in the stepsister department, in that regard.

There was no way I was going to ask Angela if she was okay. One more question like that and she was likely to loosen a couple of my teeth with a well-placed tae kwon do kick. I knew how to get her talking and it was by shuffling a deck of my recently returned cards. Out of my pocket they came and I started fanning and cutting the deck one-handed. Basically I was just showing off. While the cards had a calming effect on me, they had the exact opposite effect on Angela.

I avoided the glare and about three seconds later she was chewing her bottom lip. I sighed. She knew I knew when she did this she had something to say.

"What?" I said quietly.

She stared at my hands working over the deck and frowned.

"Do you have to do that?" she said with just the slightest hint of annoyance in her voice.

"Yes, and what?"

"Q, sometimes I just have no idea what you're saying," she said.

"You're doing the lip thing. Don't argue with me about it. It's your tell. Spit it out. Something is on your mind. If you can't say it to me, who are you going to say it to?"

She paused and looked off to the side.

"Something about Boone is bugging me," she said.

"Well, get in line, sister. There is a lot about Boone that's bugging me. Mostly how he can pull off his . . . whatever it is that he does. Which reminds me, we need to come up with a name for it, like teleporting, or something," I said.

"I thought you said it was a magic trick," Angela said.

"I did. But I don't think that anymore."

"Why?"

"Because, we've both seen it. It's not a trick or a wormhole, it's real. In a case like this, you have to look at the evidence."

"There's got to be an explanation. Maybe some new kind of technology . . . maybe X-Ray came up with something," Angela said.

"Maybe, but right now I'm working on a theory where

he temporarily hypnotizes us. Then he goes off and does his thing and plants a suggestion in our subconscious mind that he's disappeared and reappeared all of a sudden."

"How's that working out for you?" she asked with the hint of a smile.

"It still has some flaws," I said.

"Uh-huh," she said absentmindedly.

"Say it. Maybe it will help me bolster my theory."

Angela leaned forward to make sure Marie and Art were still out of earshot. "I've been thinking about Boone wearing a Nazi uniform in that old photo," she said. "What was that all about?"

"Double agent?"

"Maybe. I just wish we knew what his game was now," Angela said.

"From what we've seen, his game now is saving everyone from bad people," I said.

"Yeah. It's just . . . you know my mom, despite what she said in the cemetery. She was always kind of suspicious of Boone," Angela said.

"I think she's suspicious of everyone. Doesn't that come with the job of being a Secret Service agent?"

"I suppose. Remember how he told us the CIA recruited him right out of college? There's no way that's true. Unless he's in his eighties."

"He is pretty old," I said.

"I guess," she said. "But if he's been around since World War II . . . and everybody has said he never ages and Croc looks the same. It's just . . . too weird."

"It is. And I'm sure either he'll tell us or you'll figure it out," I said.

"Me? Why will I figure it out?"

"Because you figure out stuff. I do tricks. And I'm not going to rest until I figure out how Boone does what he does. We really need to come up with a name for it. A code word or something," I said.

"You're a magician. What about 'presto'?"

"Not bad. I mean, it does kind of fit. I was thinking maybe 'poof.' "

Angela arched her eyebrows and shrugged, clearly not as obsessed as I was with Boone's little trick.

Angela was quiet a while. "Don't get me wrong. He saved Bethany and us and all that. But if he can do this thing . . . why doesn't he take over for my mom so she's not the one in danger all the time?"

"I don't know. Maybe it's because your mom is impersonating one of the most feared terrorists in the world. We've seen him *poof* in and out of places but he's not a shape-shifter or anything weird like that. I suppose he can't change things around for her even with his power," I said.

Chief Steward Rogers returned with our food. I took a bite of what might have been heaven on a bun. It was the best burger I'd ever had in my life. If I were P.K., I would take every chance I had to fly on Air Force One and eat nothing but burgers. Burgers for breakfast. Burgers for lunch. Burgers for dinner and a midnight snack. I liked Roger. I could do worse when it came to stepfathers. But this whole vegetarian thing could be a deal breaker.

Angela sipped her green tea while I gorged myself. Hunting a super-secret sleeper cell of terrorists is hungry work and the burger, fries, and shake disappeared in about five minutes.

Just as I was about to resume our conversation, my iPhone chirped with an incoming e-mail.

"It's from P.K.," I said, looking at the screen.

The subject line read: MORE INFO FOR YOUR WH PROJECT

P.K. had cut and pasted some info on the White House in the body of his message. At the end was a link. He knew our phones were being monitored and this stuff probably wouldn't even get a raised eyebrow from X-Ray. I clicked on the link.

Up came a photo in black and white. There was a handwritten caption at the bottom of it that read, "Buffalo Bill Cody's Wild West Show, London 1902." In the front was a guy on a rearing horse holding his hat in one hand and the reins in the other. He had long blond hair and a funny goatee. He wore a buckskin jacket and pants. Behind him was a line of cowboys on horses also rearing up as the riders waved their ten-gallon hats in the air.

All except for the rider on the far right. His horse remained on all fours and his Stetson was perched atop his head. He was skinny and weathered-looking, with shoulder-length gray hair. Resting on the ground next to his horse was a very familiar-looking dog. Croc? Though it was a fuzzy image, the rider looked a lot like Boone.

I turned the screen around to show Angela the picture.

"The plot thickens," I said.

More Questions

Malak strolled to the window of the study while Miss Ruby sat behind her desk. On her way inside, Malak had taken as many mental notes of the sprawling house as she could. From the back entrance, through a sitting room, a kitchen, and a formal dining room she had finally been led down a long center hallway before walking into the library. The hallway continued on to a massive front door with a stained-glass window above it.

The window revealed an expansive front yard and beyond that pastures with more cows. There was a long drive leading up to the front of the house from a two-lane blacktop road about one hundred yards away. The drive curved off to Malak's right about fifty yards in. She assumed it ended near the giant front door, but her view in that direction was blocked by the house. The property was completely fenced in and a big gate over the entrance to the drive had words woven into the wrought iron. Reading backward, she read, "The Firebrand Ranch." Malak wondered if there was some significance to the name.

"Well, sugar pie, you must just be exhausted," Miss Ruby said. She put her feet up on her desk, displaying an elaborately tooled pair of cowboy boots. As she lit a cigarette, Malak studied her more closely. In addition to the ruby-encrusted watch, every finger bore a gemstone ring, each of them rubies, of course. She wore silver and ruby earrings the size of hubcaps. Looking at her made Malak's head hurt, but she had to admit, whether she was in Texas or anywhere else, no one would ever think Miss Ruby was a terrorist. At least not at first glance.

"That's Robert, bringing you something to eat and drink," Miss Ruby said just as the door to the study opened. The man who had driven her to the house in the ATV walked in. He was pushing a cart with a coffee pot, bottled water, fruit, cheese, and other snacks on it.

"You should sit down, honey pie, and take a load off," Miss Ruby said, the smoke from her cigarette swirling around the giant pile of hair. Robert stood next to the cart until Ruby waved him out of the study. Malak watched him as he crossed the room and closed the door behind him.

"Seriously," Miss Ruby said, the fake friendliness completely gone from her voice, "sit down."

Malak turned from the window. "I prefer to stand," she said.

"What went wrong in Kitty Hawk?" Miss Ruby asked.

"Should I call you Miss Ruby or Number Three?"

"You should answer my question."

"You should show more respect. The Leopard has claws."

Miss Ruby pushed a button on a keyboard and a monitor lowered from the ceiling. A few seconds later, Malak realized she had been right to be paranoid about being recorded. On the screen she saw herself and Number Four sitting on the couch in the Kitty Hawk lodge. Watching the scene unfold without audio was surreal, as suddenly the room exploded with action. They must have wired the house with multiple cameras, because the point of view on the screen switched and suddenly Malak was pushing Smailes toward the front door. Eben and Ziv burst through it and she fired at Eben; Smailes spun to her right from the impact of Ziv's bullet. She returned fire, knocking Ziv backward as she grabbed and shoved the now wounded Smailes through the door.

The video froze and Miss Ruby stared at her in silence.

Malak held her gaze. This was a test. She was determined not to show the slightest weakness. Malak's instincts had told her that Smailes, despite being one of the Five, had most likely never done much fieldwork. Strategy and tactical planning were his specialties, she was sure, not being in the middle of the action.

But Malak had yet to get a read on Miss Ruby. The woman owned a giant ranch and talked tough. She also looked like she could handle herself if it was necessary. Still, the Leopard had learned that in most situations her best tactic was to never show fear.

"I sense a question," she said to the woman who sat smoking, her eyes never moving from Malak's.

"Your reputation is of one who does not leave our enemies alive," Miss Ruby said, "yet you fail to kill two agents and you scurry out of the house like a frightened dog. I'm curious why you didn't finish them."

Malak threw back her head and laughed. "Do you think I am a fool? Replay the video."

Miss Ruby stayed still.

"Did you misunderstand me?" Malak asked, her eyes flashing. She was on dangerous ground. The cell had a strict hierarchy and would demand her respect. But they would also expect her to push back against any criticism of her behavior. It was a fine line to straddle.

Miss Ruby's hand moved over the keyboard and the video started again. She and Smailes on the couch . . . moving as the house was breached . . . Eben and Ziv coming through the door . . . her shooting Eben, Ziv firing and hitting Smailes in the shoulder.

"Pause," Malak said. The image froze at the point where Smailes recoiled from the impact of the bullet.

"I now have a wounded comrade between me and the two agents to my front. There are an unknown number of agents undoubtedly approaching from my rear and flanks. Training dictates a shot to the center mass of each target. Anyone who has been in the field knows every special-ops team will have body armor on all their personnel. There is no time to stop for a kill shot. And even if there were, Number Four, as you called him, is injured. We cannot allow him to be arrested, nor can I leave him behind. With a standard FBI or Special Forces tactical team, I'm facing between ten and a dozen armed men. I do not know the extent of his injury. At this very point, my obligation is now to get away with an injured comrade slowing me down, not stopping to finish our enemies."

Miss Ruby continued to look at her silently and Malak held her gaze.

"Play," Malak said.

Miss Ruby clicked another key and the video started up. It showed her shooting Ziv twice. She hoped he had not been injured seriously. Even with body armor, two .40-caliber bullets to the chest would not be pleasant. Then she nearly smiled at her concern. Ziv had sounded fine when he answered her phone call and she doubted a few bruises would slow the tough old man.

The video ended as they exited the house.

"Tell me what happened next," Miss Ruby said.

"Number Four had a boat. We took it to the mainland where an SUV was parked in a marina. He was going into shock and needed medical attention immediately. In a moment of consciousness he gave me his phone and instructions to reach a local clinic. I took him there as soon as I was able. But you already know this."

Miss Ruby smiled and clicked more keys. Another video, this one with audio, showed Malak pulling into the garage in the SUV, then the events inside the clinic, and ended with her calling the airfield.

"Why did you make two calls," Miss Ruby said, her voice flat.

"His phone dropped the call. We were in the aftermath of a hurricane. It's likely the cell towers were not operating at peak efficiency. I had to use the landline to learn the correct location of the plane."

Malak changed the subject. "What happened to Smailes?"

Miss Ruby clicked another key and the video showed the doctor working on Smailes, then the beeping sound of his heart monitor flatlining. The doctor worked feverishly, injecting Smailes's IV with more drugs and using defibrillator paddles, but to no avail. Number Four died on the table. The next few minutes of the video showed the doctor frantically gathering up his belongings, but two men dressed in black jackets and jeans, both wearing gloves, entered the building. One of them pointed a silenced pistol at the doctor and shot him twice in the chest. He slumped against the clinic wall, dead. The two men removed both bodies and the video ended.

Malak kept her face a mask, doing everything she could to show no emotion at the cold-blooded murder of the doctor. She forced herself to remember that the man had gotten himself involved with the wrong crowd. He knew the danger. But in her experience, most of the low-level terrorists she met had no real idea how brutal those above them could be.

"The doctor panicked and tried to run. There is no running from the ghost cell," Miss Ruby said. At the push of another button the monitor blinked off and disappeared back into the ceiling.

"Then there are no loose ends," Malak said, pretending to sound relieved. Now it was time to go on offense. "You are lucky."

"Lucky?" Miss Ruby said, raising her eyebrows.

"Yes. Kidnapping the president's children was a stupid move!" she said.

"Number One didn't think so." Miss Ruby sat back in her

chair and removed her feet from her desk.

"Then Number One is a fool! Taking the president's children? For what? To show them on a video broadcast for propaganda? If we wanted to strike fear in our enemies, I should have been allowed to kill them inside the White House! Instead, we ran a complicated operation with unreliable people and lost too many valuable assets. And I would expect that the president's daughter is right at this moment standing by her father's side at some press conference, her very presence mocking us. Who came up with such a stupid plan?"

Miss Ruby picked up a remote control on the desk and pointed it at a TV set in the corner. A news channel showed President J. R. Culpepper, Bethany, Roger, and Blaze along with a squirming P.K. at a podium in the East Room.

"That was earlier this morning," Miss Ruby said. "Your objections are duly noted."

Malak waited. She watched as the woman fussed and fidgeted. Lighting another cigarette, patting and adjusting her big head of Texas hair, it was as if she were struggling with a decision. Malak had no doubt Miss Ruby had been tasked with determining if the Leopard could be trusted. Finally the woman seemed to relax.

"You did well. We expected nothing less. There is another plane on its way here. When it arrives in the morning, it will take you to Chicago where you will go to a safe house and await instructions. There you'll meet Number Two," she said.

Malak was thunderstruck. She knew Angela was on her way to San Antonio. She had assumed that she would be given an assignment here. The thought of being sent away and leaving her daughter in danger was nearly more than she could bear. *Careful, Malak,* she thought. *Don't give anything away. You've come too far.*

"Is there a problem?" Miss Ruby asked. "You don't look good all of a sudden."

Malak forced herself back into focus.

"Why Chicago? Four said the next target was here." It was a lie, he had only said she was to come here to meet the others in the Five, but didn't give a reason why. It was an obvious assumption.

"There is a target here. The third SUV is on its way as we speak. But that is now our operation. Your duty is in Chicago," Miss Ruby said.

"What is the target? Please don't tell me it's another kidnapping. We must not play small here," Malak said. She paused, hoping she would get a shred of information she could pass on to Boone.

Miss Ruby shook her head. "Once you are in place in Chicago, you'll get the details. Four is dead, so Number One wants us to be extra careful. Risky as taking Bethany Culpepper might have been, it was a plan years in the making. And it came apart far too easily. Given recent events, we all voted to keep the targets and missions compartmentalized until we are ready to act."

She stood up. "Robert will drive you back to the airfield. The guesthouse next to the runway is stocked with food and drinks. You can even take a shower if you'd like. It's comfortable and will offer you privacy. Sleep well tonight and be ready to go in the morning."

Robert, who had no doubt been watching the conversation from somewhere nearby, waiting to move on the Leopard if necessary, entered the study.

Miss Ruby came around the desk and shook Malak's hand. "It's been a real pleasure, honey. I can't wait for us to meet again. Y'all have a safe trip now," she said and left the room.

Robert motioned for Malak to follow him. She left the study using every ounce of self-control she had to keep her face from showing how she truly felt. Back in the ATV on her way back to the guesthouse she could only think of one thing.

Angela.

Stranger Danger

Outside the main gate of the Firebrand Ranch, a nondescript brown sedan came to a stop. Eben was driving and Ziv was in the passenger seat. It was the worst possible setting for surveillance, with its wide-open spaces and nothing to hide behind, not even a bush. The mansion was at least a hundred yards off the road. It was in the middle of a huge parcel of flat, open land with no other houses or neighbors within miles. No doubt it had been chosen or built precisely because it would be so difficult to watch.

Neither one of them was happy now. The weather had further delayed their departure from Norfolk. Malak had been on the ground for some time. It would be dark in a few hours.

Eben popped the hood and got out of the car. He surreptitiously poured bottled water on the engine, causing steam to rise and making it look like the car had overheated. Ziv sat in the passenger seat, with the window down, trying to look like a stranded motorist. Trying and failing. The Monkey became nervous when he could not see the Leopard.

X-Ray had tracked the plane from Manteo until it had landed here. What they did not know was whether Malak had been taken somewhere else or if she was still at this location. Ziv was certain she was still close by. He knew she'd be watched closely and unable to contact him, but . . . well . . . he couldn't explain it. He could sense when Malak was in trouble and he did not have that feeling now. Not yet. Still, their position was problematic.

"This is not good," Ziv said.

"I know," Eben said.

"We can't stay here long. If we are going to do any reasonable reconnaissance, we will have to return at night."

Eben was wearing a navy-blue polo shirt, but with great exaggeration he put his wrist, now bearing the Seamaster watch, to his face. "Which will be in a few hours," he said.

"Pfft. I don't suppose your fancy watch has a telescope or binoculars, does it?" Ziv asked.

"No, but its Swiss-certified chronometer keeps virtually perfect time. Which is amazing for a mechanical watch," Eben said.

"Wonderful." Ziv got out of the car and walked to the front where he and Eben pretended to fiddle with the engine. Along the far edge of the property they saw a small ATV driving along the fence line. Undoubtedly a security patrol.

"We are too exposed," Ziv said. "A broken-down car in front of their gate while they are hosting the Leopard will not be viewed as a coincidence. We are putting Malak in danger. We must leave, call Boone, and see if X-Ray can arrange satellite reconnaissance before dark. Then we can return . . ."

"What is it?" Eben said as Ziv's words trailed off.

"Trouble," Ziv said.

Eben looked up to see a police car pulling up behind them. It rolled slowly to a stop on the asphalt behind their sedan, the blue and red lights flashing in the rising, glimmering waves of heat. When the door opened, Ziv could read the words Valiant County Sheriff's Department. He made an instant assessment of the man who emerged from the car. Mid-forties, six feet two inches tall, black buzz cut that he covered immediately with a white Stetson that had a large silver badge above the brim. He was thin and rangy looking, but his arms were roped with muscle. To Ziv he had the appearance of a man who knew how to handle himself. His gun belt contained a full complement of police equipment: mace, cuffs, collapsible baton, and, most important, a nickel-plated .357 Magnum on his right hip. He spoke quietly into the radio microphone connected to his uniform near his shoulder. So far he was doing everything by the book, Ziv thought. Which didn't mean he wasn't a member of the ghost cell.

"Good afternoon, gentlemen. What seems to be the problem?" he asked.

"We are not sure," Eben said. "At first we thought it was the radiator, but that doesn't seem to be the trouble. The car just died."

"Is that right. The car ever done that before?" the officer asked.

Ziv and Eben glanced at each other. Undoubtedly the officer had called in their plate and knew the car was a rental. He was probing them for information.

"No . . . that is, we don't know . . . it is a rental," Eben said.

"I see. And what brings you to Valiant County?" he asked.

"I'm sorry, officer . . . forgive me, I didn't catch your name?" Ziv asked.

"I didn't give it," he said, turning his attention to Ziv. "But it's Hackett, and it's *Sheriff* Hackett."

"Sheriff! How lucky for us!" Ziv said. "What a beautiful county you have here, Sheriff Hackett."

"I like it. But you didn't answer my question. What brings you to Valiant County?"

"We are just on our way back to San Antonio. . . ."

"Kind of an out-of-the-way route to San Antonio, isn't it?"

"Yes, we were lost, then the trouble with the car . . . if it starts we will be on our way. Sheriff, what an honor it is to meet you!" Ziv put his hand out and stepped toward the man.

Eben closed his eyes. This was not going to end well. No police officer anywhere in the world liked being approached without permission in a situation like this. From his years of training Eben knew that traffic stops were very dangerous situations for cops. They followed strict training protocols. Ziv should not have moved from his spot.

"Stay right there," the sheriff said loudly, drawing his revolver and pointing it at Ziv's chest.

"Oh my!" Ziv said, putting his hands up. "Sheriff, please, I did not mean to–"

"Quiet! You behind the car, step out where I can see you. Hands out to your sides."

Eben thought about turning and running but decided he couldn't because running would deny him the opportunity to strangle Ziv. So he did as the sheriff asked.

"You," the sheriff said, nodding toward Eben. "Lean forward, hands on the fender, and don't move." He turned his attention to Ziv. "I want to see your ID. Remove it from your pocket very slowly."

"Sheriff, really, is this necessary? We just need to get our car started. In fact I think we were close to correcting the problem as you pulled up. We will happily be on our way," Ziv said with a broad smile.

Eben wanted to hang his head but all he could do was grit his teeth. He had no doubt that whoever was in the house was watching what was taking place. They needed to get out of there, even if it meant getting arrested to get away from the house. Before everything fell apart, Eben offered up a silent prayer the sheriff was not an overly excitable, shoot-first-and-ask-questions-later type.

He stood up straight.

"Sheriff, my friend is right . . ." he said, choking off the words as the big revolver swung back to his chest.

"I SAID DON'T MOVE," the sheriff ordered. "Both of you. Assume the position. I'm placing you under arrest."

"On what charges?" Ziv asked.

"On the charges of failing to cooperate with an officer in lawful performance of his duty, obstructing justice, and the charge of I don't like not being listened to. Both of you on the car, now! I have a feeling you know the routine. Move and I shoot you. Don't test me," he said.

A few minutes later Sheriff Hackett had quickly and efficiently searched, cuffed, and loaded the two men into the backseat of his cruiser. After he radioed for a tow truck, they were on their way.

"We need to make a phone call," Eben said.

"You'll get your chance," barked Sheriff Hackett.

TUESDAY, SEPTEMBER 9 >

11:10 a.m. to 3:45 p.m.

A Not-So-Grand Entrance

I was going to say what a cool experience it was spending the night on Air Force One, but truthfully, I don't remember much of it. After flying to Atlanta and Tallahassee, I couldn't stay awake. I thought I'd take a short nap, but didn't realize how tired I was. Chief Steward Rogers let me bunk down in a spare bed in the staff quarters and I slept straight through to the next morning. I wasn't sure if Angela slept or not. I'd left her staring at her computer screen and that was the last I remembered until I woke up as the plane touched down in San Antonio.

Mom was still pretty geeked about flying on Air Force One. When she and Roger came on board in Raleigh, Angela had the smart idea to have them find us doing our homework. We'd updated some info on the plane and Chief Steward Rogers posed for pictures with us. Now Angela had turned to studying the history of San Antonio and, specifically, what it was probably best known for, the Battle of the Alamo, during the Texas Revolution in 1836.

Mom and Roger were happy to see us and after hugs
and greetings Marie and Art kept them busy with interview
requests and other tour stuff. With so many people coming
and going on the plane, we didn't have a chance to discuss the
pictures P.K. had sent us. Like so many other things with the
mysterious Tyrone Boone, it would have to wait. And then of
course I fell asleep.

Our San Antonio hotel was bustling, and we hadn't even
been in the lobby of the hotel for three minutes when Buddy
T. appeared. Buddy's face was a reddish color I hadn't seen
before. He'd flown down with Heather Hughes, who was
president of Mom and Dad's record company, but she was
nowhere to be seen.

"Look at Buddy's face," I whispered to Angela. "It's the 'I
had to fly on a tiny corporate jet while my clients got to fly on
the coolest plane in the world' crimson."

Finally, I got a chuckle out of Angela.

"It's about time you got here," Buddy said to Mom and
Roger. "This public service-announcement tour has thrown
off the whole schedule. If we don't—"

"It's funny you should mention that," Mom said. "Roger
and I were talking about making all the remaining dates free
in exchange for donations to the victims."

Buddy's face turned someone-just-kill-me-now white.
"Well . . . ah . . . I think if we do a little juggling we'll be fine.
It's just that a tour schedule is like dominoes. And . . ."

Buddy was now circling around Mom, who was no longer
paying attention but was instead listening to Art, who was
handing us all keys to our rooms. Mom and Roger had a suite

and Angela and I had adjoining rooms down the hall.

Buddy made his money by representing the biggest and best acts in the business. Even though he'd still get paid, he attracted more and better clients when his acts sold out auditoriums and by having his talent reach the top of the charts. If the tour suddenly stopped collecting admissions, in a couple years no one would remember that Mom and Roger gave the money to charity. It would not be a big-grossing act and that would hurt Buddy's reputation. He was a complicated, annoying little weasel of a man sometimes. But he was smart about business. The funny part was Buddy had met his match in Mom. He just hadn't figured it out yet.

About a minute after that, Dirk Peski, aka the Paparazzi Prince, arrived, shoving his obnoxious camera and his even more obnoxious self in everyone's face. The entire group reacted with groans. Angela and I—well, I wouldn't say we exactly liked Dirk, but we had learned he was Ziv's partner. And he watched the Monkey who watched the Leopard. Ziv must have gotten him here somehow.

And he had the perfect cover. The Alamo concert had changed focus. Mom and Dad had invited a couple of other acts to play with them to honor the Washington, D.C. bombing victims.

With the other artists now participating, the concert had blown up in the media and the hotel lobby was full of rock stars and celebrities. Mom and Roger had to go do interviews, so she gave me a big hug right there in the lobby.

"Mom . . . uh . . ." Dirk snapped a photo, then scurried away from our group when Art stepped in front of him and cracked his knuckles a couple of times.

"Sorry," Mom said. "Didn't mean to embarrass you. It's just this past day has been so . . . well, my head is spinning! Air Force One and the album doing so well and . . . I try not to forget about the bombing victims but . . ." her words trailed off as she put her hands on my shoulders, looking me over and giving me the "mom inspection." From the corner of my eye, I saw Roger doing the same thing to Angela. I guess it was a universal parent trait.

"Mom," I said. "Don't feel guilty. You've earned this and you deserve it. You and Roger are doing a great thing to help people."

She kissed me on the cheek again. "You're so sweet. I wonder where Boone is? He called me and said he was going to have a couple of guys he trusted drive the coach and he'd catch a flight. He heard about the concert adding the other acts so he wanted to get here quicker and make sure everything was on schedule," she said, switching the subject abruptly. "Maybe you and Angela should come to our suite until . . ."

"Howdy."

I almost jumped, and over Mom's shoulder I saw Angela's eyes grow wide. Boone was standing right in front of us in the bustling lobby.

"Boone!" Mom said. "I was just asking about you. . . ."

"I know. My plane was late gettin' in yesterday. All kinds of air traffic delays 'cause of that storm. You know how much I like flyin', anyhow. Had to take a long walk around the city this mornin' just to calm myself. And I wanted to stop off at the Alamo stage and make sure the roadies got everything squared away for tonight," Boone said.

Boone could drop in and out of his drawl as easily as he dropped out of thin air.

"How's the crew?" Mom asked.

"It's good, Blaze. Had to stop some monkeyin' around. You know how roadies get sometimes. Ain't a one of 'em don't think he's gonna be the next Bobby LaKind," he said.

Mom chuckled. She knew a lot about music and music history.

"Who's Bobby LaKind?" I asked.

"Bobby was a roadie for the Doobie Brothers," Mom said. "They were a huge act back in the seventies. One night after a show, some of the band members caught him playing the conga drums. Turns out he was a real talent and eventually he became a full-fledged member of the band."

I knew that most roadies got into the business because they were or wanted to be musicians. But I'd never heard of a roadie making it into a band before. Being a roadie was hard, unglamorous work.

"Yeah, I knew ole Bobby," Boone said. "Did a couple of tours with the Doobies back in the day. Rest easy, Blaze. Ain't no Bobby LaKinds in this bunch. But they're doing a good job. Now, I figure you and Roger got all kinds of work to do, so don't worry, I'll take care of Q and Angela."

"Okay. But Q, are you keeping up with your schoolwork?" Mom asked me.

"Sure," I said, smiling.

"Q . . ." Mom gave me the half stink eye.

"No, seriously, we are. On the plane we did a report about

Air Force One and we were learning about the Alamo and stuff . . . about Texas . . . and hurricanes . . ." I was almost in big trouble. Angela did the homework. I'd been too busy trying to do Boone's magic trick. I had no idea what our homework situation was. But I tried to sound convincing, hoping Mom wouldn't ask too many questions.

Angela came to the rescue. "I couldn't help overhearing, and you know what? The Alamo is really a fascinating story. I'm looking forward to working more on it," she said. "I'm hoping Boone will have a chance to take us over so we can get some photos and video for our assignment. I was just reading this morning about the actual battle. There's a lot of controversy over how many men died there. Historians argue between a hundred eighty-three and one eighty-five, depending on who—"

"One eighty-four," Boone cut in.

All of us looked at him.

"I read a lot, ya know?" he said. When he looked at Angela and me, I was pretty sure he winked.

"Anyway," Angela continued, "is it okay if we hit our rooms? I think we'll finish our assignment and, I don't know about Q, but I could use a nap." Angela was likely going to be the best secret agent ever. She could stretch the truth to the breaking point and make you believe every word of it. So far the only person she hadn't been able to crack was Boone. Forget the fact that she'd forgotten I'd just slept for about a zillion hours and didn't need a nap.

"Sure," my mom said. "Roger and I will go do our press stuff so that Buddy T. doesn't have a meltdown before we get any further behind in the schedule. We'll check in with you later. Keep your phones on, both of you!"

Boone followed us to our floor.

"I've got the SOS crew in a room at the other end of the hall. I need to check in and get an update. I don't have any new information yet, but they might. Stay tuned . . ." He took off down the hall.

Once in our rooms, I opened the adjoining door and fiddled with my deck of cards while Angela got her laptop booted up.

"What now?" I asked. "And please don't say homework."

"Yes, you've got to be exhausted from all the homework you've been doing," Angela said with a sly smile.

Ouch.

Angela looked at the screen and pulled up the pictures of Boone. I'd forwarded P.K.'s e-mails to her earlier.

"Can you send a message to P.K.?" she said. "Tell him thanks for the photos. And ask him if he can find any more."

Gearing Up

Boone entered the three-bedroom hotel suite that SOS had turned into their command post. X-Ray had four different laptops and several high-definition monitors on two desks and a coffee table. Boone was never sure what X-Ray was doing, but knowing X-Ray it probably involved hacking some secure federal database. Felix was over against a wall in the sitting area doing one-handed push-ups and watching ESPN. Beyond him, Vanessa had brought a board from the intellimobile into the suite and was practicing her knife throwing. Uly was in one of the bedrooms, sleeping.

"Where have you been?" Vanessa asked.

"I had some things to check out," Boone answered. "X, what's the story on the SUV?"

X-Ray nodded in the direction of one of the monitors. A grainy image of the empty warehouse, with the lonely vehicle parked in the center, occupied the screen.

"The cell put in a wireless camera to keep an eye on the SUV. I was able to piggyback the signal. The battery on the tracker only has another couple of hours of juice left. It's probably too risky to try to sneak in and put on a new one. But I've hacked into all of the traffic cameras in the city and I'm working on the external security cameras on most of the major buildings within a twenty-block radius of the warehouse. Should have access in another few minutes." X-Ray chuckled. "People think they can go buy a router with encryption from Radio Shack and their wireless signal is secure. What a joke." He said it almost gleefully, which would have worried Boone if X-Ray weren't incorruptibly honest.

"What about Malak's plane?"

"I sent the GPS coordinates of where it landed to your phone," X-Ray said. "It's about thirty miles southeast of the city. I'm working on getting satellite coverage. The address shows a place called the Firebrand Ranch. Big place. Private airstrip. I'm running records on it now. So far I see it's a bunch of corporations owned by other corporations, owned by shell companies. Wouldn't have expected anything less."

"All right. Be ready," Boone said. "We have no idea what's going to happen with this vehicle. I haven't heard from Ziv or Eben in several hours and that worries me. Their calls go to voice mail. X-Ray, once you've got views on all the streets around the warehouse, start looking for signs that they've got people watching. If we have to send somebody over there, I don't want anybody running into countersurveillance. Call me if you need anything." He left the room.

He went back to Angela and Q's room and knocked on the door, Croc at his heels. Angela let them in. She didn't look happy.

"Okay, here's what we know," Boone said as he entered the room. "X-Ray found where your mother's plane landed. Eben and Ziv aren't answering the phone. So I need you to hang out here. I'm going to go check on Malak."

Angela was wound up tight and I thought she was about to unload on Boone.

His phone's chirping stopped her.

"It's J.R.," he said, looking at the caller ID. "Hey, J.R."

Angela and Q could hear J.R. talking extremely loudly. Even from across the room they could recognize his voice. Boone listened and said, "Got it" before hanging up.

"All right," Boone said. "We've found Eben and Ziv."

"How does J.R. know where Eben and Ziv are?" I asked. "And where are they?"

"He gave Eben a Seamaster. And they're in jail. C'mon, Croc." They headed toward the door.

"In jail?" we both said at the same time.

"Yep. J.R. checked the jail records and they've been there since yesterday afternoon. Something is up. They should have been allowed to make a phone call and would have called one of us."

We'd taken our watches off before we got on Air Force One so Roger wouldn't see them. J.R. had also given one to Malak when she was an agent. Roger would have immediately recognized them. My watch was in the pocket of my cargos and Angela's was in her pack. I'd forgotten all about the tracking devices J.R. had put inside them. Frankly, it creeped me out a little to think the president of the United States could find me anywhere at any time as long as I kept that watch on me.

"Hey, Boone?" Angela said, "you know that picture of the German officer we showed you, the one with the dog who looked a lot like Croc?"

"Yeah," he said, turning at the door to look at the two of us.

"Did you ever fight in the war?"

"Which one?" Boone asked. "I've fought in a lot of places." I stared back and forth between them, wondering who would break the tension first.

"Why are you asking now?" Boone asked. His tone was suddenly scary.

"No reason," Angela said. "Just, that picture looks an awful lot like you. And so did this one from Buffalo Bill's Wild West Show." She turned the laptop around so the screen was facing him. He walked closer, squinting to look at it. I watched him for any sign of deception but the old spy betrayed nothing. He had no tell.

"Where'd you get that?" Boone asked.

"Just stumbled across it doing some research," Angela said. "Looks kind of like you, doesn't it?"

Boone looked closer at the photo. Then shook his head.

"Nah. Maybe a little. Been around a long time but never met Buffalo Bill. That dog does look an awful lot like Croc, though, I'll give you that. Listen, I've got to go. We'll talk about this later."

"You lied to us about being recruited by the CIA out of college," Angela snapped. "You told us you'd tell us the truth, now you've been gone for hours doing who knows what. And we've seen you and Croc go *poof* . . . who are you, Boone?"

He stopped at the door, his hand on the knob, and looked back at us. I saw Boone's shoulders sag ever so slightly.

"Poof?" he asked.

"I came up with it," I said. His eyes narrowed as he considered it.

"Look. I was gone for hours . . . because . . . I just . . . there was something I had to do. I don't have time to talk about this now. But don't worry. I'll be back in a flash." He stepped into the hallway with Croc at his heels and closed the door.

I had no doubt he would.

The Leopard Stalks

Malak could not stop pacing. She'd spent the night taking short naps, sitting on the floor of the small living room, at the far end of the couch. It would give her a clear shot at the door. Miss Ruby had undoubtedly reported her debriefing of Malak to the rest of the Five. There was a chance they'd decided she had become a liability and would terminate her.

She didn't think so, but she was in a new arena now.

Malak knew it was paranoid. But it was how she planned to stay alive, by leaving nothing to chance.

The building next to the airstrip was small, air-conditioned, and stocked with food and drink. But she couldn't concentrate on any of that now. For years she had devoted her life to destroying the ghost cell by rooting out its members one by one. Seeing Angela in Washington and again in Kitty Hawk had thrown her off her game. It was causing her tremendous heartache and she was losing the battle of will she must win to keep herself alive.

The image of a leopard stalking back and forth in a cage

was not lost on her. She shook her head, trying to clear it. This building felt like a cage to her. The air conditioning was not keeping pace with the rising Texas heat. She went to the window facing the airstrip and cranked it open slightly. A little breeze blew in but did little to cool down the interior.

Still trying to keep her emotions in neutral, she went into the small bathroom and opened the faucet. The cool water ran over her hands and she dabbed some on her face. It helped a little. The mirror revealed a Malak Tucker she barely recognized. Though she frequently changed hairstyles, the nervous energy she was burning every day had given her face a much leaner look.

She studied the Omega Seamaster watch on her wrist, given to her by President Culpepper. After the explosion at Independence Hall, she removed the tracking device inside it. In her role as the Leopard, J.R. could not know she was alive or where she was. But how many times in the last few days had she considered calling the engraved number on the back of it? *Just reach out to him and let this all be over. You've done more than your share, Malak Tucker,* she would say to herself. J.R. assumed the watch had been destroyed in the explosion. Up until she had taken Bethany from the White House, he had no idea she was even still alive. But though he could no longer know where she was by tracking her watch, she *could* always call him. Why didn't she?

Because she still had a job to do.

When she came out of the bathroom, she visibly started. Boone was sitting in the overstuffed chair next to the couch, which Croc now apparently claimed as his own. By reflex she reached for her pistol, and Boone held up a hand to stop her. "Easy, Malak," he said.

Malak let out her breath and relaxed from the adrenaline rush she'd just experienced. She knew the guesthouse might be bugged or that a camera might be monitoring the building, so she stayed in character as the Leopard.

"What are you doing? Who are you? Did Miss Ruby send you to check on me?"

"Relax, there's no one listening," Boone said, holding up his phone. "X-Ray gave me a little app doodad that can detect bugs, cameras, and wireless signals. Plus I think every time I use it I get a free coffee at Starbucks. Even better, Croc would know if anyone was listening."

Malak relaxed a little but was still angry. "Are you insane? What are you doing here? How did you even get in here?"

"Malak, you have to trust me. Croc and I have been doing this a long time. Over the years, we've . . . gained the ability . . . and know-how . . . to get around all kinds of alarms, security patrols, and every kind of surveillance you can imagine. And now X-Ray helps too," he said, waving his phone in the air. "So, relax. Seriously, we're safe unless someone walks in, and before that happens, Croc will know. I believe in X-Ray and I trust Croc even more when it comes to this stuff."

"That old dog? How could he know if this place is wired?" Malak broke cover. If Boone was wrong, she figured, the place would be swarming with guards by now and apparently no one had noticed.

Croc opened one eye and looked at her, then immediately closed it.

"That's his insulted look, by the way," Boone said. "What have you learned?"

"How's Angela? Is she all right?"

"She's fine. Perfectly safe. She and Q are in the Westin, doing homework. The SOS team is four doors down; two operatives are with Roger and Blaze in their suite. Everyone is fine, Malak, you have my word."

Malak felt better. She would never stop worrying about Angela but the news was comforting. Despite her initial reservations about him, she knew Boone was very good.

"I'm being sent to Chicago," she said. "I don't know why. They had me wait here overnight. They must be waiting on pilots, or else the same flight crew needed downtime or something. I'm to go to a safe house and wait for instructions. I'm supposed to meet Number Two there."

"Huh. Chicago," Boone said. For a few seconds he was silent, apparently lost in thought.

"What is it?" Malak asked.

"That's where Match is headed next. I wonder why they're sending you there."

"I don't know. But I don't like it. I want you to pull Angela off the tour. Quest too. Come up with some excuse. She's in danger, Boone, and I'm losing my ability to focus. That could get a lot of innocent people hurt."

"It could. But Malak, I know you. When the moment strikes, you're one of the most focused people I've ever met. We're close now. They know we're watching but in the last few days it's almost like the ghost cell doesn't care anymore. I don't think they know who exactly is watching but I think they've made some kind of connection between Philadelphia and D.C. and now they're shadowing us. If I pull Angela and Quest off now and send them home, if I do anything that looks remotely suspicious, they could fade away and it might be years before we find them again. We can't let up yet."

"I don't like it," Malak said. "This is my daughter."

Croc raised his head, his ears twitching.

"Someone's coming," Malak said, her hand going to the pistol in her waistband.

Boone stood and looked out the room's window.

"Car coming. Must be your pilots," he said.

"I still don't like this, Boone."

"I know. But I promise you Angela is safe. And we can finish this. We're closer than we've ever been. I'm asking you to trust me."

"All right. I go to Chicago. You stay with Angela. But so help me, Boone, if I get a sense that anything is going wrong or Angela is in danger, I'm pulling the plug. Do you understand me?"

"I do. I'd suggest you go outside and meet the pilots so no one comes in here and finds me. One more thing. Pat Callaghan will be running countersurveillance on you until Eben and Ziv arrive."

Malak gave him a grim stare. She was relieved to have Pat watching her back, but didn't like putting another friend in danger. It wouldn't surprise her if he had volunteered.

After a moment her face took on a curious expression.

"What?" Boone asked.

"You look tired, Boone. When is the last time you slept?"

she asked.

"I got a lot of rest yesterday after I left North Carolina," he said.

"Really. Well, you must not be sleeping well. You seem . . . different," she said.

"It's just the heat," Boone said.

"Boone. You're responsible for my daughter's safety. If you're not totally focused . . ."

"I'm fine," Boone said. "You need to get going."

Malak's eyes narrowed and she gave his face the once-over again before she left the building. A few minutes later, the car slowed to a stop and the same pilots from the previous day emerged from the backseat. They gave her a curt nod and began immediately to ready the aircraft for takeoff. The car drove away.

When the plane was ready, Malak boarded. The aircraft taxied into position and a few minutes later it accelerated down the runway and into the air. The Leopard was on the move again.

Inside the guesthouse, Boone stared out the window at the mansion off in the distance. Croc stood and ambled off the couch. They both stood there in the room for a moment. And then they were gone.

Always Watching

Just as the plane lifted off, a dog started barking outside the mansion. Loudly. Then it started to howl. Miss Ruby, sitting at the desk in the study, stood and went to the window. Outside she saw a dog. It was hard to tell from the distance, but it looked like a blue heeler, rolling around on the ground and barking. It was off to the side of the driveway, about fifty yards from the road. It came to its feet and shook its head back and forth, lifting its head to the sky and howling. And from where she stood, it looked like it was foaming at the mouth.

"Oh, no. A rabid dog," she muttered. Retrieving a small two-way from her desk, she pushed the button.

"Robert, there's a dog out front by the road goin' wild. Looks like it might be rabid. Call the county animal control and then check it out, sugar," she said.

"Copy. On my way to the front door now."

Miss Ruby went back to her desk and sat. A few minutes later, the dog raised another horrible ruckus.

She returned to the window and pulled back the drapes.

Robert and two other men were standing where she had last
seen the dog. She could hear it barking like crazy, but she
couldn't spot it anywhere.

"Oh, for heaven's sake, they better catch that thing before it
gets into the pasture with the cattle," she muttered. Retrieving
a pistol from the desk, she left the study.

As soon as she exited the room, Boone walked in. The
study was just off the main hallway that led to the front door.
He was going to have to be quick.

The tracking device X-Ray had given him before he had
left the hotel was the size of a hearing-aid battery. Boone had
seen a lot of things in his day but it never ceased to amaze
him how such things were becoming smaller and smaller. He
wanted to find something that Miss Ruby was likely to take
with her if she left the ranch, but her purse wasn't here and he
didn't have enough time to search the house.

Smoke curled up from a cigarette she'd left burning in the
ashtray. On the desk next to it was a jeweled cigarette case.
Boone pried it open and found a nearly full pack of cigarettes
inside. He removed them, put the tracking device at the
bottom of the case and the pack on top of it. Snapping it shut,
he heard the front door open and voices in the hall.

It was time to go.

The Sheriff

Boone entered the Valiant County sheriff's station, which was fairly quiet on a Monday afternoon. From the outside it looked a lot like every small-town police station Boone had ever been in. There was a two-truck fire station attached to the south end of the building. At the back of the parking lot, a small building stood off by itself. A sign over the door read: Valiant County Animal Control. In front of the building was a black van. Dogs could be heard barking and howling inside the structure, causing Croc's ears to prick up. Boone smiled at the thought of criminals and wayward dogs held at the same compound. He'd always believed if people loved and took care of dogs, there'd be a lot fewer criminals in the world.

The inside of the station was also familiar. A big wooden counter sat perpendicular to the front door. A desk sergeant working away on some paperwork occupied a stool behind it. Beyond that were four metal desks grouped together, one of them occupied by a deputy questioning a handcuffed man seated in a chair.

"No dogs allowed," the desk sergeant said as Boone and Croc entered the station house. The sergeant looked up quickly, instantly dismissed Boone as anyone important, and returned to his task.

"He's a service dog," Boone answered. The sergeant looked up again. He studied Boone with a skeptical eye.

"Service? For what?" he demanded.

"Anxiety. I need to see the sheriff," Boone said.

"Why?" The desk deputy had now turned his attention to Croc.

"Because he has a couple of people in custody and I'm here to get them out," Boone said. The deputy tried to give Boone a hard look and failed. Boone's ponytailed gray hair and deeply lined face were impervious to intimidation.

"The sheriff is busy. Have a seat on the bench and he'll get to you as soon as he can."

Boone nodded to Croc as if signaling something, then sat on the bench, his long legs stretched in front of him, crossed at the ankle. Croc paced in front of the desk right below the officer's nose. It only took a few minutes.

Scratching his pen over the reports, the desk sergeant suddenly looked up. He looked to his right and left and even behind him as if at first not understanding what was happening. Taking a manila file folder off the desk, he covered his nose with his other hand and waved it back and forth.

"Is that your dog, mister? Are you sure it ain't sick? It smells like . . . like something . . . died!" He slipped off his stool and stepped back from the desk. The file folder was now a blur.

"I'm sorry, I don't smell anything. I'm just waiting to see the sheriff so I can be on my way," Boone said.

It didn't take the sergeant long. Still covering his nose, he grabbed the phone on his desk and pushed a button, muttered something into the receiver, and hung up.

"The sheriff is right down the hall," he said, pointing to Boone's left.

Boone stood up. "Come on, Croc."

Sheriff Hackett's office door was open. Three glass panels to the left of the doorway made it appear a little brighter inside. On shelves behind his desk Boone spotted several trophies for pistol shooting, a small replica of a Bradley Fighting Vehicle, and the assorted photos and certificates that every county sheriff in America possessed.

"May I help you?" the sheriff asked.

"I think so. My name is Boone. I understand you arrested a couple of men outside the Firebrand Ranch yesterday afternoon. I'm here to pick them up," he said.

Sheriff Hackett leaned back in his chair and studied Boone. "I did take two men into custody yesterday afternoon. Imagine my surprise when I checked the IDs they were carrying and discovered they were from Homeland Security. Agents James and Younger?"

Boone knew X-Ray had given everyone various multiple sets of IDs but he couldn't be sure which ones Eben and Ziv had used.

"Yes. James and Younger," Boone said, making a mental note to instruct X-Ray not to create fake IDs named after famous outlaws. "Is there some reason you took them into custody?"

"Well, since I've never met you before in my life, let's just say I didn't like the way they looked, Mr. Boone. By the way, I don't suppose your first name is Daniel, is it?" the sheriff asked.

Boone shook his head.

"No? Anyway, I also found two really interesting duffel bags in their trunk."

"But as Homeland Security agents–" Boone began.

The sheriff held up his hand and removed a sheet of paper from an open file on his desk. "I don't know many Homeland Security agents who carry a police uniform, two sawed-off shotguns, four 9-millimeter Beretta pistols, two Colt .45 Desert Eagle automatic pistols, a MAC-10 pistol with thirty mags of ammunition, two sets of brass knuckles, a bowie knife, four canisters of mace, an M-4 automatic rifle with five clips of ammo, six canisters of tear gas along with a tear-gas gun, two collapsible batons, a cattle prod, a bayonet, and two stun guns. I also checked passenger manifests for all commercial flights into San Antonio in the last three days. I don't have any passengers named James and Younger arriving. But I suppose a couple of Homeland Security agents would have their own air transport, wouldn't they?" He put the sheet down and glanced at Boone.

"They never know what their nation will require of them," Boone said.

"Uh-huh," the sheriff said. "Doesn't look right to me."

"Surely their credentials checked out," Boone said.

"Oh, yes. See, that's what I was working on right now. They're in the federal database. Both of them are quite decorated. But when I call to verify their identities, no matter which number on their profile I dial, the same guy answers. He tries to change his voice. But it's the same guy."

Boone's face showed nothing. He needed to tell X-Ray to change the phone contacts in the database so the verification calls were directed to Vanessa. She was a talented mimic and could pull it off. X-Ray was a technical genius but a horrible liar.

"Sheriff Hackett, I can assure you–" Boone said, but the sheriff interrupted him again.

"I don't know who you are. Or who those two men are. But no one is going anywhere until I get this sorted out, and in fact–" The phone on his desk rang. He glanced at the phone, then hollered through the open door to the desk sergeant.

"Dang it, Mack! I said no calls!"

"I didn't put one through!" the sergeant shouted back.

The phone kept ringing.

"I think you might want to answer that. And put it on speaker," Boone said.

Hackett looked at Boone, then at the caller ID on the phone screen, and his eyes grew wide. He pushed a button on the phone. Before he could even say anything, a voice came over the line.

"Sheriff Tom Hackett?"

"Um. I . . . uh . . . yes. Who is this?" Sheriff Hackett asked.

"This is President J. R. Culpepper."

"I . . . um . . . hello? Mr. President?"

"Do you have a question, Sheriff? I'm sure you recognize my voice, don't you?"

"Yes . . . sir. I . . . recognize your voice," he stammered. Sheriff Hackett sat up straighter in his chair.

"Good! The man across from you is Tyrone Boone. Older guy, gray ponytail. Sort of looks like Willie Nelson?"

"Ah. Yes, sir, that's him," Sheriff Hackett replied.

"Excellent. He works for me. So do the two men you have in your jail. I'm going to need you to release them," J.R. said.

"Um. Mr. President, I'm . . . I've . . . I'm in a bit of a pickle here. They had a whole trunk full of weapons and if word gets out I let . . ." Sheriff Hackett said.

"Boone? You going to tell anyone?" J.R. asked.

"Don't see why it would ever come up," Boone said.

"I'm certainly not going to mention it. So there you go, Sheriff. Problem solved."

The sheriff stood up at his desk now. "Mr. President, with all due respect—"

"Sheriff. I've looked into your background. I know you did two tours in the Middle East. You are, in fact, a highly decorated marine. Your marksmen scores are quite impressive and your service record book shows you were a squared-away jarhead, with outstanding performance appraisals across the board. *If* it were up to me, I'd tell you everything. But I can't. All I can say is that these men are part of a vital national-security initiative. And I can't have them eating bologna sandwiches and solving Sudoku puzzles in your jail right now. You have my word that if this causes you any grief, politically or any other way, I will do my very best to give you cover for it. I'm afraid that will have to do. Now, can you get my men out of your jail for me?"

"Yes, sir, Mr. President," the sheriff said.

"That's great. Really great! I appreciate this, Sheriff. You have no idea. Boone?"

"Yes, J.R.?" Boone said.

"I'm by myself in the situation room again. My staff is about ready to cut through the door with a torch. I've got to get out there before they call Congress and invoke the Twenty-fifth Amendment. Call me as soon as you have any news," he said. The phone line went dead.

Sheriff Hackett looked at Boone. Then he looked down at Croc, who was curled up at Boone's feet. It was almost as if he was noticing both of them for the first time.

"You call the president of the United States of America, 'J.R.'?" He was incredulous.

"That's his name," Boone said.

The sheriff put his hand on his forehead and ran it over his buzz cut. He let out a long sigh.

"All right," he said, "let's get your men."

A few minutes later the desk sergeant was handing Eben and Ziv two big envelopes with their personal effects. They dumped their wallets and keys and a few other items on the countertop and began to fill their pockets.

Eben peered into his envelope and shook his head. "Where is my watch?" he asked.

The desk sergeant, unsure of exactly what was happening, shook his head.

"I don't know, sir," he said.

The sheriff came down the hallway with two large duffel bags. He put them on the floor next to Boone.

"I sure hope you and your special cargo have a safe trip. Out of my county," Sheriff Hackett said.

"We won't be troubling you anymore, Sheriff," Boone said.

"There will be trouble if I don't get my watch in the next thirty seconds," Eben said.

"Stop fussing over your watch like an old woman," Ziv said. "It is unbecoming."

"Sheriff. When you arrested me, I had a very nice watch on my wrist. It is not with the rest of my personal effects," Eben said.

"It wasn't that nice," Ziv muttered.

"It is an Omega Seamaster," Eben said.

The sheriff, no longer amused, held up his hand. "Wait here, Agent Younger. I locked your watch in my office. Let me get it." He returned a few minutes later with the watch in his hand.

"Thank you, Sheriff." Eben grinned broadly as he strapped his prized possession on his wrist. He looked at it admiringly and held it to his ear, to hear it tick. Ziv muttered a curse under his breath and grabbed the duffel bags, storming out of the station. Eben followed after him, whistling.

Boone put out his hand. Hackett shook it but didn't look happy about it.

"Thank you, Sheriff. And thank you for your service to our country," Boone said.

"Yeah. Right. Good day, Mr. Boone," the sheriff said, turning on his heel and storming down the hallway to his office.

A New Crew

The door to the warehouse opened and four men strolled in. The white Tahoe was parked in the middle of the empty space. Two of the men took up positions at windows next to the front and rear doors. The glass was clouded with dirt and grime. Each man carefully wiped away just enough of the gunk to see out but not enough to make the window look as if it had recently been cleaned. The ghost cell was obsessive about details like this. *Do not leave any sign for your enemies to follow.*

The men wore jeans, cowboy boots, and long-sleeved oxford shirts with the sleeves rolled up to their elbows and the shirttails untucked. They all wore cowboy hats, which were as numerous in Texas as the bluebonnet flowers that grew nearly everywhere. It would be important that they fit in later. The four young students who had driven the SUV from the East Coast had faded back into the shadows. These men were not like them.

None of the men referred to one another by name. They had never met, had no previous connections, and did not need any such information to complete their mission. They had been put in motion by an anonymous text, telling them to meet at a coffee shop six blocks away, then take separate routes to this location, making sure they were not watched. The text said something harmless and innocuous, like an everyday message sent between friends . . .

> I'll meet u @ Cup O' Joes. Order me a 4-grain bagel. If u get coffee 2 go, b careful. It's always hot.

The text gave them the meeting place. The four-grain bagel reference indicated that there would be four operatives. The phrase "hot coffee" meant that when they received instructions on where to go next, to watch for tails or any countersurveillance.

Now one of the men approached the Tahoe while the others stood back. This was the man Number Four had told Malak about. It would be his job to inspect the timer and make sure it was still functional. Of the four, he was the longest-serving cell member and he had created many such weapons in their long and glorious struggle.

They had not searched for video or audio bugs in the warehouse. If they used an electronic sweeping or jamming device, they risked setting off the bomb. All of their cell phones had been powered down to avoid accidental detonation. If someone were watching and the police arrived, they would have to try to escape into the San Antonio streets.

The man removed his cowboy hat and cautiously opened the back window of the Tahoe. It was packed with C-4 plastic explosives. The timing device was close to the rear of the vehicle. Very carefully he shone a small flashlight beam on it. Its panel light was green, so it was still getting battery power. When the Tahoe engine started, it would recharge the battery to full capacity. He could see that each of the detonator wires looked secure and there were no loose leads.

He dropped to his knees and looked at the shiny aluminum box welded to the gas tank. The device, which Uly had spotted earlier, was a kill switch. If necessary, and once the timer had been activated, someone who held the proper device could enter a code and transmit a signal to this box and disarm the bomb. He inspected each wire attached to it. They were all securely fitted in place.

The man figured that unless there was a short in the electrical timer itself, everything looked good. The bomb should work perfectly. As he rose to his feet, he did not see X-Ray's now dead tracking device, as it was hidden from his view by the vehicle's bumper. He looked at his watch.

"Time to go," he said. Retrieving the keys from the front driver's-side tire, he climbed into the Tahoe and started it up. Two of the men joined him inside the SUV as the fourth pushed open the door leading out onto the street. Once through, the door was closed and all four were soon securely inside and accelerating down the street.

As they turned the corner at the first intersection all the traffic and security cameras in a three-mile radius went offline.

TUESDAY, SEPTEMBER 9 ›

4:45 p.m. to 9:45 p.m.

What to Do About Boone

Boone had gone off to do whatever it is Boone did, and a short time later, Felix and Uly knocked on our door. Boone had told them to take us out and let us explore some of downtown San Antonio. At first Angela said she wanted to stay in the room.

"Boone says we're to get you out, for fresh air and education," Uly said.

We had sort of gotten used to Felix, who was scary in his own right. Uly was a near mirror image of Felix and just as imposing. Angela and I both decided we would enjoy a walk. Outside. For fresh air. And education. And because Uly said so.

The walk actually was kind of refreshing. Uly and Felix kept their distance, unless we stopped to look in a store window or read a historical plaque. If someone paused next to us or wanted to read the same plaque we did, the two men stepped up right behind us, invading the other person's space and nearly blocking the sunlight. Usually the person took one look at the two of them and scrammed.

The space right in front of the Alamo looks kind of like a park, with lots of trees and walkways. It was abuzz with activity as equipment was being loaded onto the temporary stage in preparation for the concert. We watched for a few minutes as the roadies moved amplifiers and lights and all the other things you needed to successfully stage a concert. I'd seen it all before, but it was still interesting to watch.

The stage was right in front of the Alamo. All of the modern equipment was a stark contrast to the weathered walls of the mission.

While Angela and I watched, Uly disappeared into the Alamo Visitors Center. Felix stood behind us but didn't say anything. A few minutes later Uly came back and he was holding four plastic badges on lanyards.

"The Alamo is closed to tours because of the concert, but Boone arranged for us to get passes."

"How did he do that?" Angela asked.

Felix shrugged as he placed the lanyard around his neck. "Boone knows people."

We went to the gate, where a guard looked at our passes and waved us through. We walked inside one of the most famous places in America and were completely alone. The feeling was . . . haunting.

I guess I didn't know what to expect about the Alamo. It's something you've always heard about but you don't really have a sense of what it's like until you actually see it for yourself.

Angela was looking at the brochure. " 'There were more than 180 men who died here trying to defend it against thousands of Mexican soldiers. The Mexican Army laid siege to the Alamo for several days before they finally attacked on the morning of March 6, 1836,' " she read aloud.

" 'At the beginning, the defenders turned back two attacks, but the third time they were overwhelmed and it was over in a few minutes. The most famous men who died there were Colonel William Barret Travis, Jim Bowie, and David Crockett,' " she continued to read.

I couldn't say what it was, but there was something about the place that really hits you when you walk through it. For one thing, it's a lot smaller than I expected. In my mind, I thought it was like this big fort.

"A lot of people think it was this huge place. But it's essentially a building just like many others that Spanish monks built throughout Mexico and the southwestern United States. They were places for Spain to convert Native Americans and organize and control their settlements. During the Texas Revolution, the Texians—as they called themselves then—fortified the Misión San Antonio de Valero to try to slow down General Santa Anna's march through Texas. They were trying to buy time so the Texian Army could gather enough volunteers to stand against his vastly superior numbers and win their independence," Angela said.

"I thought it would be bigger," I said. "Being surrounded by all the huge modern buildings in downtown San Antonio makes it look even smaller."

It was weird because as we walked through the place, read the signs on the displays, and touched the walls, all of us, even Uly and Felix, were silent. It's almost like talking was disrespectful somehow. I'd never been in a place quite like it in my life.

In the sacristy, a small room inside the mission walls, there's a little sign that tells how the women and children who were there during the battle hid in that little room. General Santa Anna spared their lives and told them to spread the word to the rest of the rebellious Texians about what happened there to those who attempted to oppose him. Only it backfired.

"The survivors did tell what happened," Angela said. "And hundreds of the Texians were enraged and rushed to fight under General Sam Houston. They crushed General Santa Anna at the Battle of San Jacinto a few weeks later and won their freedom from Mexico. Barret, Bowie, and Crockett went down in history as martyrs to the cause of freedom."

Later, as we headed back to our hotel, Uly and Felix gave us our space and Angela and I were quiet as we strolled along. The Alamo is a place that stays with you for a while after you visit it.

Uly and Felix dropped us off at our rooms and we tried to kill time. The longer we waited for Boone to show up, the more restless Angela became. She started pacing. Like she was trying to break the world record for stalking back and forth in a hotel room. I was sitting on the bed shuffling my cards. I couldn't think of anything to jolly Angela up. I was about to ask her if she wanted to see a card trick, just to see the response, when we were interrupted by a knock at the door.

Angela opened the door. Croc scurried in ahead of Boone and hopped up on the bed right beside me.

"I just got back from my . . . errands," Boone said.

I slid a little farther back on the bed to get away from Croc, who smelled like he'd been working overtime in the Disgusting Odors factory.

"Is my mom okay?" Angela asked.

"Your mom is fine. She met with Number Three, a woman who goes by the name of Ruby Spencer and owns a big ranch south of here. Malak has been sent on to Chicago to a safe house. Eben and Ziv are on a flight to Chicago and they'll pick up surveillance. Apparently the cell has plans there but we don't know what yet."

"Who is going to watch her? She always has Ziv and Dirk and . . ." I could tell she was trying hard to keep the worry out of her voice but she was only partly successful.

Boone held up his hand. "X-Ray is tracking her jet. Right now Agent Callaghan is in the backseat of an F-14 Tomcat and almost to Chicago. He's going to pick up her trail and watch her until Eben and Ziv arrive. After that he's going to run countersurveillance on them and the safe house. Pat is good. Almost as good as your mom. It's covered."

Angela relaxed a little.

"With an assist from Croc, who played rabid dog at the ranch, I got inside Ruby's house and placed one of X-Ray's tracking gizmos in her cigarette case. If we need to, we can find her—as long as she takes her smokes with her. I just checked in with J.R., so everyone is up to speed."

"Boone, we've got all kinds of questions . . ." Angela started to say.

"I know you do. And I've told you what I can. When this is all over, I promise you I'll tell you everything. But it's a big story and we really don't have time to deal with it right now," he said.

Something was different in Boone. Or maybe it wasn't and all along it was just something I'd been too busy to notice. It was a little over a week earlier that Boone had "found" us in the middle of Nevada. One morning I had just stepped out of the coach. There I found Boone camped out with a sleeping bag, a little stove, a big heavy pack, and his stack of James Bond paperbacks. But since then, I didn't remember seeing him sleep. I'm sure he must have, but I just don't recall it. And right at that moment, he looked tired. No one else would probably notice with his thick beard and weathered skin. But I wanted to be a magician and to do that you had to be super observant. Tyrone Boone looked like someone who could use a nap.

"But Boone, you've got to see it from our–" Angela was interrupted by the beep of Boone's phone.

He held up a finger. "Hold on, it's X-Ray," he said, then spoke into the phone. "All right. What? Where are Uly and Felix? Did you get any hits? Okay. Download those photos to everyone's phones. I'll be there in a minute. Get those cameras back up, X." He snapped his phone shut.

"Four new guys just showed up at the warehouse and got into the SUV. We've got photos of each of them. When this new crew pulled out in the Tahoe all the traffic cameras in the surrounding area went down. We need a special satellite because of the cloud cover, and J.R. will order one to be repositioned to help us. But it takes time to move them into place. X-Ray is trying to get the cameras back up now. You two stay here. I'm leaving Croc with you."

He started toward the door.

"Wait," Angela said, "we can help."

"No. Not until I know it's safe. I promised your mother nothing would happen to you. You both stay in this room. Don't leave and don't try anything fancy with your phones. You know you can't take the batteries out, right?" He was serious.

"Boone," Angela tried whining. "Can we at least go to the restaurant to eat? We've done a lot today and we're hungry."

"No restaurant. Order something from room service if you want. I mean it, Angela. No tricks. You too, Q."

"I'm good," I said.

Boone opened the door and for a second I thought my eyes were playing tricks on me. Because I was pretty sure that before the door closed all the way, Boone had disappeared.

I was still staring at it and heard Croc whine a little. I looked at him and found him staring back at me with his blue eye. The brown eye was shut.

Getting off the bed, I hustled to the door and opened it, peering up and down the hallway. Boone was gone.

"Poof!" I said.

TUESDAY, SEPTEMBER 9 >

3:45 p.m. to 10:15 p.m.

Waiting

At the Firebrand Ranch, Miss Ruby sat at the desk in her study, smoking a cigarette and biding her time. As she rubbed out the butt in the ashtray, the smartphone sitting on her massive desk chirped. She had been waiting for the call, unsure what her instructions would be. As the phone chirped, several thoughts flashed through her head.

She had been Number Three in the cell for some time. It was a cause she had devoted her life to. In the last two days she could not escape the feeling that something was . . . different. Number One had been giving commands, making plans, and essentially co-opting control of the group to the point that Ruby felt as if she and the entire cell were in danger of exposure.

When the Leopard arrived earlier in the day, almost her first words were to challenge the kidnapping of Bethany Culpepper from the White House. In Miss Ruby's mind, the Leopard lived up to her reputation. During her debrief she appeared smart, capable, and cunning. She brazenly called the decision to take the children as well as the president's daughter stupid, and in truth Miss Ruby could not disagree. It had been a huge risk and had in fact blown up in their faces. As the Leopard had remarked, they had lost numerous valuable assets.

Normally, they would fall back now. It was how they always operated. Whether the objective was met or the mission failed, the ghost cell said nothing, took no credit, and showed no public face at all. There were plenty of terrorist groups just waiting to claim the notoriety for themselves, and when they did, it provided the ghost cell with cover to operate unnoticed.

But now, someone was noticing them. To Miss Ruby it felt like they were foolishly exposing themselves and taking too many unnecessary chances. After the SEAL team rescued the president's daughter, Miss Ruby argued for retreat and a chance to regroup. Now that Number Four was dead, Anmar, the Leopard, was officially a voting member of the Five but it appeared those above her in the cell's hierarchy were not quite sold on the Leopard's loyalty and had ordered her to Chicago almost immediately. Miss Ruby did not believe in luck. But with the unsuccessful attempt to kidnap Bethany Culpepper, and the failure of the two car bombs to destroy any meaningful targets, it made her feel like something was up. It was the only thing she could think of to describe the feeling. Her instinct was to wait. Recover. Let a new plan take shape. But those above her wanted to press forward.

Miss Ruby thought this was madness. She argued her case with Number Two. But Number Two almost always voted as Number One wished, like a loyal lapdog. In her view,

Number Two was mostly useless but, as second in line, had the ear of Number One. And besides, the cell was structured as it was structured. She could air her views, but in the end she followed orders.

And truthfully, while she thought Number Two to be a competent planner and tactician, there was something about Number One that made her . . . uneasy. If someone asked her to identify why or what it was that made her feel this way, she was certain she would be unable to put it into words. They had only been together in person a few times, but each meeting had left her looking over her shoulder for days afterward, as if she might find Number One suddenly there.

On the last ring, before the call went to voice mail, she answered.

"Howdy!" she said sweetly.

"Hey! I guess it hasn't shown up yet, but did you ever find out about the package?" She recognized the voice. Number One.

"I did, sugar. It's in San Antonio but the company tells me it's not out for delivery yet."

"Oh, shoot! I was hoping it would be there by now. It's a special gift and I really wanted you to have it before the night is over."

"Well, no worries. We were planning a trip into the city anyway. I told them to hold it for me and I'll swing by and pick it up," she said.

"I hate to trouble you," the voice said.

"Oh, it's no trouble, sugar. I'm grateful to have it. Really, it is far too generous. You shouldn't have," she said sweetly.

"But I did. I'm glad you're going to get it. Let me know what you think when you pick it up," the voice said as the call disconnected. There was a tone in the last sentence that told Miss Ruby it was an order and not a request. *Let me know when you pick it up*, she thought. It was clear to her she did not have a choice. She was going to San Antonio.

Miss Ruby put down the phone. The conversation had gone the way all forms of electronic communication went between cell members. To anyone listening, they could be talking about a delivery of flowers, a birthday gift, or a box of steaks on dry ice. No one outside their circle would have any indication of the meaning behind the words.

On her desk sat a small console for an intercom that ran throughout the sprawling house. She pushed a button. "Robert, Sean, Marco, get in here."

A few minutes later the three men filed in. Robert and Sean were identical twins, six-two and built like bodybuilders, their black polo shirts barely fitting over their chests and bulging biceps. They had wide faces crisscrossed with scar tissue from fights and other violent incidents. The only way Miss Ruby could tell them apart was that Sean's poorly healed broken nose listed slightly to the left.

Marco was shorter and leaner, about five-ten, and his features were sharp, giving him an almost rat-like appearance along with his dark and angry eyes. Each of the men had been with her for a few years and she trusted them to follow her orders without question.

"We've got a pickup to make. Get everything ready, like we planned."

The men left the library and went off to gather what they would need for their next task.

Miss Ruby shuddered. What they had planned shouldn't be dangerous at all. But she couldn't help feeling that they were about to make a horrible mistake.

She leaned back in her chair and lit another cigarette. There was time for one more smoke before they left. In truth, she ought to give up the nasty habit.

It would probably kill her one of these days.

Chasing Ghosts

When Boone reached the intellimobile in the hotel garage, X-Ray and Vanessa were nearly ready to roll. Boone had lived a long time but it never ceased to amaze him how quickly X-Ray could move his seemingly endless stacks of equipment from any hotel or motel room, or wherever they were set up, into the van in a matter of minutes. His fingers flew over a couple of switches and keyboards and in seconds he had the monitors up and running and could call up a visual of just about anything. It was a marvel to Boone.

The old roadie slid into one of the seats in between Vanessa and X-Ray, who handed him a Bluetooth headset. He slipped it into his ear. "Give me an audio check," X-Ray said.

"Felix, Uly, where are you?" Boone asked. X-Ray gave him a thumbs-up, signaling the headset was working perfectly.

Felix's voice came back. "The SUV is in the wind. We're three blocks out from the warehouse and circling in a large radius. We've been looking for a roost where someone could sit and run countersurveillance, but so far there's nobody hiding, as near as we can tell. Do you want us to go search the warehouse? It's at the end of a dead-end street and difficult to approach without being seen, but we could give it a try."

Boone swiveled his seat to look at a monitor showing a map of the area surrounding the warehouse. It was in a fairly quiet part of town, but a few blocks from a couple of surface streets that led to freeways. The SUV could be anywhere by now.

"What about the tracker?" Boone asked X-Ray.

"No good. The battery is dead. I can get Felix and Uly inside the warehouse, if you want. See if they left anything behind," X-Ray said, looking up at a monitor showing the now empty interior.

"No. We can't waste the time," Boone said. "Felix, Uly, head back toward the concert. It's the biggest event going on right now. It's the logical target. But don't assume that all four guys will stay with the vehicle. Get eyes on every white SUV in the vicinity that you can. Start rolling now."

Boone's eyes bore into the map of downtown San Antonio. With the crowd control and streets blocked off for the concert, everything was out of sync. In the older city center, streets ran at odd angles and crisscrossed everywhere. There were literally a half-dozen points where a car bomb could wreak havoc in a big way.

Of course the ghost cell could be sending the SUV somewhere else. But Boone didn't think so. He believed they knew someone was watching them. Or at least they suspected it. They would think the government was looking for the SUV even if they weren't hearing any chatter about it on police scanners or through their own network. Boone and his crew had rescued Bethany Culpepper without anyone outside the cell and the SOS knowing. Keeping the hunt for a single SUV quiet would be easy compared to that. It could be they had decided to take it off the board and hide out for a while. But he doubted it and he didn't have time to consider the cell's master plan. There was a car bomb somewhere in San Antonio. The only safe assumption was that they would deploy it where it would do the most damage.

That meant the concert or something near the Alamo was the target.

"All right, everyone, listen up. Felix, when you get back here, grab the sniper rifle and get on the roof of the Emily Morgan Hotel. It's going to give you the best view of the traffic approaching the concert. Uly, Vanessa, and I are going to patrol the area around the concert crowd, starting with the perimeter. We'll work our way in toward the stage. I've got a feeling at least a couple of them will be in the crowd or somewhere very close by."

"Copy that," Uly said.

Boone opened the side door of the intellimobile.

"Where are you going to be, Boone?" Vanessa asked.

"I'll be around," he said.

Room Service

"Poof," Angela repeated. She threw herself back on the other bed.

"Yep," I said.

Croc had completely taken over the second bed and I had no desire to share that space with him. So I moved to the armchair in the corner.

Angela sat up. "You know what? I've got to do something. I can't sit here like this."

"But Boone said . . ."

"I know. I'm not going anywhere. Physically, at least. But we can still dig into Boone's background. I can't stand not knowing. So if he won't tell me, I'll just start looking myself. Send another text to P.K. and ask him if he's found anything yet. He's got better resources than we do. Just tell him we need more WH info if he finds anything interesting. That will sail by X-Ray."

I knew better than to argue with Angela so I sent another text. Angela sat at the desk and flipped open her laptop. Before

long she was lost in something she'd found on the Internet. I
don't know if it had to do with our homework, Boone, or if
she was pulling up a schematic of the hotel to find a way out
through the ventilation system.

Croc sat up now and cocked his head. He made a series of
strange sounds. Not exactly whines or growls, but he jumped
down off the bed and was now staring at me and huffing and
pawing at the chair.

"What's got into him all of a sudden?" Angela asked.

"Beats me," I said. Croc usually slept most of the time.
Now he looked a little agitated.

"Just out of curiosity, do you suppose he's had all his
shots?" I asked as he edged closer to me.

"I would think. Boone seems very attached to him. I don't
expect he'd allow Croc to get sick if he could avoid it," Angela
said.

"The way he's looking at me is creeping me out a little."

Angela retrieved the room-service menu from the desk
drawer and sat down on the corner of the bed opposite me.
I was practicing more cuts and shuffles with a deck of cards.
There was a small table in between the two beds where the
room phone rested.

"What do you want to eat?" Angela asked.

"Burger, fries, milkshake," I said.

"Q!" She laughed. "You better hope my dad doesn't check
the room-service receipts. He does that, you know."

"I'm willing to risk it."

"It wouldn't hurt you to eat a salad once in a while," she
said.

"Lettuce and tomato on my burger, please."

"They have salads that look really good," Angela insisted.

"Go ahead. Order one."

"Oh, all right, burger for you it is," she muttered. As she reached for the phone Croc was suddenly there; he gently knocked her hand away with his muzzle. She reached again and he did the same thing.

"Stop it, Croc," she said absentmindedly, still studying the menu. Again, as her hand went for the handset, Croc pushed it to the side.

"What is up with him?" Angela asked.

"Obviously he doesn't want you to order salad."

Croc positioned himself against her legs and each time she tried to reach the phone, he interfered with her in some way. Always gently, but still preventing her from using the telephone. Finally Angela couldn't take it anymore and grabbed his collar. She walked him into my room and shut the adjoining door. Croc scratched at the door and whined.

"Hey! I have to sleep in there tonight! Do you know how stinky it's going to be?"

She ignored me.

"That is weird. I've never seen him act like that before," Angela said. She sat back down on the bed and picked up the phone and placed the order.

A few minutes later, while Croc scratched and whined, it came over me.

The itch.

I'd been doing a one-handed cut of the deck and it just hit me. The itch is a feeling I get every once in a while. It's not exactly precognition or anything like that. I can't tell *what's* going to happen, only that something *is* going to happen.

The last time it happened to me, Croc had been there. And he'd been acting all strange then, too, barking at the truck Malak and Bethany were riding in when I thought he had just gone nuts. Now he was weirding out again and I had the itch. There are no coincidences. But like I said, I never know exactly what to do with the itch and it doesn't necessarily mean something bad is going to happen. Not true. Something bad almost always happens. Otherwise I'd probably never notice.

A few minutes later, with Croc still scratching and whining from the next room, there was a knock on Angela's door. When she opened it, a room-service waiter was there with the food on a cart covered by a floor-length tablecloth.

The waiter pushed the cart into the room.

Before the door could swing shut, a woman with the most bleached-blond hair I'd ever seen, followed by a guy with a gun, stepped inside the room. Both of them were wearing press credentials and had cameras around their necks. The hotel was crawling with media types so it was probably a pretty good cover.

"Well, aren't you two just as cute as little bluebonnets. I'm pleased to meet you both. My name is Ruby Spencer."

Taken for a Ride

Everything happened fast. The waiter who was not a waiter pulled a gun out of his waistband and pointed it at me. Now all of them had guns. And he was big. Like juiced-out-on-steroids, crush-your-skull-like-a-walnut big.

With both of us covered, Miss Ruby smiled and dropped her pistol into a purse hanging from her arm. The purse was roughly the size of Delaware and bedazzled with bright red rubies. With her rings, jeweled purse, blond hair, and all that mascara and rouge she looked like a big, blond, sneering devil.

"Over-accessorize much?" Angela said.

Miss Ruby ignored her insult.

"Well now, sweetie pies . . . let's just everybody stay calm and friendly like," Miss Ruby said.

It didn't take Angela long to get her back up. "What do you want? Who are you?" she demanded. The "I'm about to go all tae kwon do on you" look was in her eyes. I'd seen her take out Eben in Philadelphia with a kick. She had a black belt. But these guys had guns. Guns that were in their hands and pointed at us.

"Angela," I said calmly. There was no way she could do anything now. A room-service cart was standing between the bad guys and us. Not to mention it was really close quarters. Any move she tried was probably going to get her shot. And me. Which would really impair my ability to do card tricks.

"What do you want?" she demanded again. Angela. Only she would get bossy with armed terrorists.

"What I want right now, sugar, is for y'all to calm down. There isn't a need for anybody to get hurt. Now Miss Ruby's going to take your li'l brother here on a nice ride is all. And y'all going to stay here with Marco and behave like the fine young lady I know you are," Miss Ruby said.

"You're not taking Q anywhere," Angela said. Yay, Angela. Hold that thought.

"Darlin', I'm afraid you don't have a choice," Ruby said.

"Over my dead body," Angela said.

"Honey, that can be arranged," Miss Ruby said.

The men took silencers out of their pockets and screwed them onto the muzzles of each gun. It was like it was happening in slow motion. And the effect was chilling. I felt like my body weighed ten thousand pounds and I couldn't move.

Fake Waiter produced some plastic flex-cuffs and waved me toward him with his gun. I so wanted to shuffle my deck of cards right then because I was unbelievably nervous. Reaching for them was probably not a good idea. He motioned again for me to move. Finally, I was able to get my legs working and took a step toward him.

"Don't move, Q!" Angela said.

"Honey, if you don't keep your voice down I'm afraid we'll keep it down for you. Now, Q, you be a good boy and get on over here. Nobody is going to hurt you. Move it," Ruby said to me. This last sentence was more a command than a suggestion.

They had the guns so I did what they said. Crossing the few feet of the hotel room felt like it took hours. The next thing I knew, flex-cuffs were slipped over my wrists and pulled tight.

Miss Ruby was behind me. I was trying to look at Angela to make sure she was okay and that she wasn't going to do anything that might get us both killed, when I felt something sharp poke me in the neck. I tried twisting and struggling to get away, but Fake Waiter yanked on my cuffs and held me in place. A kind of burning feeling crawled under the skin on my neck, then traveled across my chest. Seconds later my head felt weird, like it was full of cotton or something. I was suddenly dizzy and just wanted to lie down.

Ruby tossed a syringe into the trash can.

"What did you do to him?" Angela shrieked. Her voice sounded like it came from far away.

"He's going to be fine. Just a little something to relax him. Now, Q, you be an angel and crawl underneath this tablecloth," she said. She was holding the tablecloth up, showing a metal shelf beneath the cart. I knew I shouldn't, but it was like I didn't have control over my own body. When I sat on the bottom shelf of the cart and the tablecloth dropped into place, I should have been angry or thinking about escaping or whatever. But I just couldn't make my limbs work. No matter how hard I tried.

"Q! Wait! What did you give him?" Angela shouted again. The only thing I could focus on was that the tablecloth was a really ugly shade of yellow. Then I heard the door open and the cart started to move.

Under the Gun

Angela stared at the man with the gun. He removed the camera and press credential from around his neck and tossed them onto the bed closest to the door. Her eyes were like laser beams burning a hole in him but he didn't seem to care. He was a little over six feet tall, with black hair, dark eyes. He was pretty buff, Angela noticed, and looked like he knew how to handle himself. Despite her best efforts, giving him the stink eye had no effect.

He waved his gun toward the chair in the corner next to the TV. "Sit down," he ordered.

"No." She crossed her arms.

He raised the gun and pointed it directly at her. "Now."

She figured she'd better do what he said, and slumped into the chair. There wasn't any time to waste. If she couldn't think of a way to get rid of this guy, Q was probably dead. Ruby had said Q was going to be fine. If the cell had tracked them or was watching them somehow, why did they take Q away and leave her here?

"Got a phone?" the guy asked her.

She shook her head. "My dad won't let me have one. Thinks they are the harbinger of the complete collapse of our civilization," Angela said.

"Wow. That's too bad," he said. Raising the pistol, he pointed it at her again. "Don't lie to me. Where is it?"

She pointed to the desk where she'd been working on her homework. The phone lay next to the computer. If he walked past her to pick it up, she might be able to . . . but he wasn't falling for that.

"Get up slowly. Drop it on the ground and stomp on it."

Angela tried very hard to show no reaction. But Q was getting farther away by the second. She had to think of something quick.

Angela retrieved the cell, dropped it to the carpeted floor and stepped on it, cracking the glass screen. She moved back to sit down, but the guy was not convinced.

"No," he said. "In pieces. Smash it up real good."

There was no way out of it, and she did as he requested.

The man sneered at her. "Now sit back down," he said. He leaned up against the door leading to Q's adjoining room. Angela remembered Croc was still in there. And she recalled how Croc had reacted when Speed Paulsen had surprised them on the coach.

Her momentary lift in spirits was dampened when she realized she was thinking a tired old dog could save her. Besides, she'd never get the door open. Boone and Croc could do some weird stuff but she was going to have to get herself out of this. And she didn't have much time. She'd have to get free and find Boone somehow.

Minutes went by and the tension was almost more than she could bear. The gunman stood like a statue. The cell members were well trained. He stayed perfectly still but was always watching her, and she could tell he was ready to react in an instant if she tried anything. There had to be a way out of this. She started thinking about her mother, Malak, and how she had infiltrated the ghost cell by making everyone believe she was her own sister, aka Anmar, the Leopard. Angela knew that no matter what, she couldn't give up.

She nearly jumped when someone knocked on the hallway door to the adjoining room.

"Housekeeping! Turn-down service," the voice said.

The gunman straightened. He looked at Angela and put his finger to his lips in warning. As if to emphasize his point, he pointed the gun directly at her. He backed up and put the chain lock on the entry door to her room.

Angela could hear the housekeeper moving about in Q's room. She wondered what the person thought when they spotted Croc, probably stretched out on the bed snoring and smelling up the place.

A few more minutes went by. Angela heard the hallway door to Q's room shut and a few seconds later came the knock at the door to her room.

"Housekeeping! Turn-down service," the voice said.

The gunman put his finger back to his lips again. Angela wanted to shout but the barrel of the gun was only a few feet away. The guy would never miss at this range. A few more knocks, then she heard the beep of the master keycard being inserted in the lock.

The door came open a crack before it caught on the chain.

"Oops! Sorry!" The door clicked shut and Angela could hear the housekeeper move on to the next room. The gunman resumed his stance and stared at her like a snake.

"How long are we going to stay here?" Angela asked. If she could get the guy talking maybe she could get under his skin and needle him into making a mistake. Or at least get information out of him.

The guy didn't answer.

"Why did you take Q and not me?"

"Shut up," the gunman said.

"Did they leave you behind because all you can handle is teenage girls? Haven't worked your way up to adults or old people on walkers yet?"

The guy didn't respond but Angela detected a brief glint of anger in his eye.

"Yep. You guys are like the bravest terrorists ever. Setting off car bombs in shopping malls or parks so you can kill a bunch of innocent people. You appear to be really talented at kidnapping thirteen-year-old-kids like Q. I'd love to see you go up against someone who could actually fight back, like . . . oh, I don't know . . . a circus clown or a—"

"I told you to shut up," he said, gritting his teeth and pointing the gun at her again.

Angela took a breath. She hadn't figured out yet what he was waiting for. The cell had snatched them both before, but now just Q. Was he waiting for instructions?

It was the slight movement that drew her eye, otherwise

she might not have seen it. The patterns and colors on the bedspreads nearly camouflaged him. Sticking out from underneath the bed closest to the door and farthest away from her, but shielded from the gunman's vision, was a dog's muzzle.

Croc.

What's Happening to Me?

There is a trick to getting out of flex-cuffs or any kind of restraint. Actually it's two tricks. I happen to know both. You don't need to dislocate your shoulder or anything fancy. Or keep the key or a paper clip under your tongue or up your sleeve like you would for regular handcuffs. Though it would be helpful if flex-cuffs used keys. Or a knife. It would be faster at least. Actually, I don't know if a knife or key would be faster. The knife probably. But possibly the key.

Whoa. Whatever they injected me with was . . . wait a minute. At first, I'd felt all woozy and dizzy when they'd given me the shot. Now whatever drug they used had my brain working even faster than it did when I was nervous. Miss Ruby said it was supposed to calm me down and make me sleepy. Instead I was wide awake. And hyped up. My heart felt like it was going at about two hundred beats a minute and my thoughts were flying through my head so fast I couldn't keep track of them all. Something was wrong with my senses. I thought the drug should dull them, but instead they were magnified somehow. Noises were louder. Lights were brighter. Maybe I was allergic or she had missed a vein or it didn't . . . It wasn't working right.

I wasn't calm or sleepy like she planned. It was doing exactly the opposite, acting more like a stimulant. What if I *did* have some kind of allergy or something? I know I had a reaction once to penicillin when I had tonsillitis. It gave me a really itchy rash and it didn't cure me, so the doctor had to give me something else. What if I was having a weird response to this drug and it wasn't affecting me like it was supposed to? I really needed a deck of cards to shuffle so I could figure this out, but my hands were otherwise engaged behind my back.

Once we had gotten off the elevator in the parking garage, they pulled me out of the bottom of the cart. There was a big black SUV close to the elevator door and they dragged me along to it. Then it occurred to me—the fact the drug wasn't working like it should was a good thing. But Miss Ruby and her minions should probably remain ignorant of that fact. So I shouldn't tell them. In fact, I should pretend like it *was* working, I decided.

They shoved me into the backseat. I was told to keep quiet and not to try anything smart. No problem. Even though my brain didn't feel sleepy or tired, my arms and legs felt kind of rubbery.

I landed in a heap on the backseat but instead of complaining, I giggled.

"Don't worry," Fake Waiter said to Miss Ruby. "Whatever you gave him has really hit him. He's totally out of it."

Excellent. I'm a magician, I kept telling myself. A magician practices deception.

As the car pulled out of the parking garage, it turned left. When Angela and I had been passing time on the coach, she told me some of the things her mother taught her about being a Secret Service agent. Angela called these things "tradecraft," sort of an umbrella term used to describe the methods an agent used in the field. Tactics such as how to blend into a crowd, how to properly conduct countersurveillance, and also things you could do if you were ever abducted.

One thing was to try and look for passing landmarks. Even if you were in an unfamiliar place, you could look for unusual buildings or anything that would allow you to mark the direction your kidnappers were taking you. But I couldn't really see anything lying as I was on the backseat. I tried counting the number of seconds between turns, but that didn't work either because the SUV went slower on the surface streets, and then we must have gotten on the freeway because it really picked up speed and went a long way without turning and I lost count. Besides, I figured Angela would eventually get word to Boone. Or at least I hoped she would.

I was pretty sure we were headed out of the city and probably to Miss Ruby's ranch. Miss Ruby didn't know Boone knew where she lived. Once Angela got to him, he'd come and get me. Right now, I had to concentrate on making them think I was helpless.

I guessed we'd driven for about a half hour and then slowed, made a turn, and rolled to a stop. A few seconds later Fake Waiter opened the back door, then yanked me off the backseat and onto my feet. It kind of hurt, but the drug was supposed to be making me not feel stuff, so I didn't wince.

Instead, I giggled. "Waiter, did you exer give me myze hamburger? Because I'm shtill hungry," I said slurring my words and smiling at him like a dope.

He shoved me hard in the back toward the front door of a big house. It was dark outside now and off in the distance I could hear cows mooing and assumed this must be the ranch.

"Hey, *doan* be sho mean," I said. "I just . . . do I smell cows?"

Neither of them answered me, but Fake Waiter shoved me again.

"Where are we?" I said, weaving around like my knees might buckle at any moment. "And hey . . . you *didn't* bring myze dinner! I'm hungrys and . . ."

"Shut up if you don't want another shot," the guy said and gave me a third shove in the back. This time I pretended to get my feet tangled up and fell down on the ground. It was hard to fall gracefully with my hands behind my back and I skinned my knee a little bit.

"Ows! Thaz's harsh, dude," I said. I had been around Speed Paulsen enough in my life to know what somebody sounds like when they're stoned. I thought I was doing a good job.

"Take it easy, Sean," Miss Ruby said. "We're not supposed to hurt him."

Fake Waiter's name was Sean.

The jolt of pain when I fell to the ground kind of brought me closer to normal from the effect of the drug. I could think a little more clearly now. Not supposed to hurt me? Why? I wondered. Ransom? Probably not. The cell didn't do things for money. And if they wanted ransom they would have taken Angela too.

It was weird. For the life of me, I couldn't figure out what they wanted or even how they knew where we were staying. I knew Boone was worried about Malak's real identity being uncovered by the cell. If her cover were blown it would put Angela in danger. But it didn't seem like they'd figured out Malak's connection to us yet. If they had, they probably would have just killed her already. And if they had discovered her deception, and even if they'd tortured her to learn what she knew . . . well . . . I'd met Malak up close a couple of times in the past few days. And I didn't think she could ever be tortured into revealing her identity, if for no other reason than to protect Angela. She would die first. I suppose that they could have found out about her some other way. And maybe they'd taken Angela to some other location to keep us separated. That way they could sit back and wait to see who came after us and discover who was tracking them.

If they knew Angela was Malak's daughter, maybe they were trying to set a trap for the Leopard. If she came to Angela's rescue they would know for sure. But if they harmed Angela in any way, they *would* have to kill Malak because she would never stop until she hunted down every single one of them. So there was that.

"You won't give us any trouble now will you, Q, sugar?" Miss Ruby cooed.

She needed to work on her manners because when she said "sugar" it sounded totally insincere.

"Do I shmell cows?" I said. "I like shugar. Do you have some?"

"How much of that stuff did you give him?" Sean asked Ruby. "He's babbling like an idiot."

Ha. That's what you think. You just wait until . . . I . . . you just wait. I was pretty sure whatever Ruby had injected me with was really wearing off because my mouth was getting dry and I was getting a headache. This worried me a little bit. What if I really was having an allergic reaction of some kind and was going to suddenly develop really serious symptoms? It happens.

Once inside, they led me into this big study or library full of a lot of floor-to-ceiling bookcases and big leather chairs and couches.

Sean cut my flex-cuffs and my hands came free. With his hand clenched around my neck he guided me around the big desk and shoved me into the chair. Miss Ruby stood in front of the desk. After lighting a cigarette, she took a really big puff and blew out the smoke. It traveled through the air over the desk and whirled all around me. I was pretty sure she did it on purpose.

Miss Ruby removed an iPhone from her purse. Her fingers worked over the screen and she put it to her ear.

"We're good," she said. "You have the order," she said a few seconds later and disconnected the call.

"What are we going to do with him?" Sean asked. Right then another guy walked in. He looked exactly like Sean, but wasn't dressed like a waiter.

"Robert," Miss Ruby said. "I just gave Marco the order."

"Hey, waiter guy," I said, looking at Sean with one eye closed. "Did youse know there is shombody elshe here who looks exactly like you?"

As Sean looked at me, his eyes narrowed. "Shut up," he said.

"You are so grouchy all the time. You want some of myze hamburger?" I looked around at the desk and the floor to either side of me, my head flopping about. "Where did myze hamburger go?"

Robert and Miss Ruby laughed and she put the phone down on the desk. I wondered who she'd called. I hoped Marco wasn't the guy they'd left with Angela and now they were going to . . . I didn't want to think about it, but I was pretty sure I knew what "you have the order" meant.

I couldn't let them see the worry in my face, so I let my head loll forward and hang with my chin against my chest. I knew Angela was devoting every ounce of the brain- and willpower and energy she had to getting away. I had to do the same. I owed it to her.

My eyes zeroed in on Miss Ruby's phone. She had an iPhone with no case, just like me. I hadn't gotten around to getting a case since my phone was replaced. As a terrorist she was probably switching phones all the time and didn't bother with a case. Although I wondered if she realized she was missing a chance to cover something else in rubies. How useful would that phone be to Boone once X-Ray got hold of it? If I could switch it out with mine . . . I just couldn't stop my thoughts.

"We're going to wait," Miss Ruby said. "Sean, empty his

pockets."

Sean came around the desk and lifted me to my feet. He pulled open the Velcro flaps on my cargo shorts and emptied all of my stuff out onto the desk. The decks of cards, my ropes, silk scarves, baseball cap, sunglasses, and, most important, my iPhone. All the stuff clattered across the desktop. I stared at my phone, which had landed just a few inches away from Miss Ruby's. So close. Then he removed my Omega Seamaster. My Seamaster! Please, J.R. Please be monitoring our whereabouts right now and come get me.

"What is all this crap?" Sean complained as he emptied my last pocket, the one containing my magic coins.

"Mashick," I said, continuing to slur my words.

"Can I has a glash of whater?" I asked, my head still bobbing forward like I might fall asleep at any moment. I raised my head and gazed at Miss Ruby with one eye closed like I was trying hard to focus.

"I don't see why not," she said. "Sean, why don't you get our guest a glass of water?"

Sean didn't look happy, but he left the room. Now all I had to do was stall and give Angela or J.R. a chance to call in the cavalry.

And figure out a way to get my hands on Miss Ruby's phone.

Making a Move

Angela tried to slow her breathing. Croc's muzzle disappeared back under the bed. She had no idea how he had gotten from the adjoining room or what he was up to. She tried hard to think of how to get away or at least shout for help or something. She had seen Croc in action on the coach when Speed Paulsen stumbled out of the master bedroom. If she could divert the gunman's attention just long enough . . . and then his phone rang. Without taking his eyes off Angela he pulled it from his pocket and answered.

"Yeah," he said. Then a few seconds later he said, "Understood."

And as it turned out she didn't have to do anything to help Croc. The gunman left his spot by the adjoining door and stepped closer to her. He raised the gun, the silencer on the end of it now only a few feet from her.

"Sorry, kid," he said. "If it's any consolation, I kind of like your spir–" He never got a chance to finish, because Croc launched himself from somewhere behind the gunman and his jaws clamped down on the thug's arm. He screamed in surprise and shock.

To Angela the sound of the lowlife shouting for mercy sounded like music. Her mother had told her that oftentimes people in situations like this one tended to see real-time events in slow motion. It was a way for their brains to put a limit on the flow of information and process what was taking place. Her mother also said people who possessed this ability were more likely to keep their cool in tense situations. And this is what was happening to Angela.

The gun spun wildly in midair. Without hesitating, she was up and out of the chair and moving toward the door. Partly to get away, but also to get clear of the gun in case it accidentally discharged when it hit the floor. But it clattered away under the bed.

Croc's momentum at first carried the guy forward toward the room's window. But Angela made note that the old dog was extremely agile for his age. He twisted his neck and body in midair. His weight and the fact he had his teeth firmly planted in the guy's arm allowed him to face-plant the gunman on the bed.

"Get off, get off me!" He tried punching at Croc with his free hand, but kept missing because Croc was never in one spot more than an instant. To Angela he even looked different, just like Q had said. Younger and more agile, with a mouth full of teeth. Sharp teeth. Not a single blow was landing on the dog. Angela thought the creep looked like he was trying to swat a swarm of bees. Croc bit him on the back of the neck and started in on his ears, his calves, his hands, moving like a blur.

Angela was on the way toward the door, when she spied the camera on the first bed, where the guy had tossed it. Croc was still biting, snarling, and growling but the man was getting his legs under him and trying to rise.

For the gunman, his bad day was about to get a lot worse. For just as he got to his feet—with Croc still making like the dude was the world's biggest dog biscuit—Angela swung the camera with all her might. It connected flush against the side of his head, and he dropped to his knees and slumped over on his side.

Out cold.

"Good boy, Croc," Angela said. Her breath was coming in short gasps and she hugged the dog hard. Sitting as he was on the bed, he was almost as tall as she and didn't seem to mind the hug one bit. In fact, he gave her cheek a nice long lick with his tongue. It did more than anything else to snap her back to reality.

"Ack. If you hadn't just saved my life," she complained mockingly, wiping dog drool off her cheek. Croc stared at her with his blue eye, his tongue sticking out through the empty spot in his mouth where his teeth were missing. She couldn't deny what she'd just seen. But she sure as heck didn't have an explanation for it.

"How did you do that?" she asked. Croc just stared at her and blinked his blue eye—almost like a doggie shrug. Angela had never had the chance to be around dogs much but there was a part of her that thought Croc understood everything she was saying. Which was, of course, impossible.

"Okay. Got to think. I have to call Boone." With her phone in pieces on the floor, she went to the room phone, but as she reached for it her arm stopped in midair. It suddenly occurred to her that she didn't know Boone's number. Or anyone's on the SOS team. The numbers were all preprogrammed into their phones. She knew her dad's but she couldn't call him. She had to hurry. There was no telling how soon the guy would wake up. And if he got away or got word to anyone, Q was probably dead.

Croc waddled across the bed and stared at her. She wondered if maybe he was hurt and reached out to pat his head. As she did, Croc pawed at her wrist.

"What are you doing? You keep doing that. Stop it. Are you okay?"

She reached for him again and this time his head moved really fast and he took her wrist in his mouth but he didn't bite down.

"Croc, gross! Let me—" Then she got it. Her wrist! Where she would normally be wearing a watch. A very special watch given to her by the president of the United States. One that she kept in the pocket of her backpack because she didn't want her dad to see the same watch her mother had worn and start asking questions. Her Omega Seamaster.

"Old and smart," she said, digging the watch out of her backpack and dialing the number etched on the casing with the room phone. A familiar voice answered on the third ring.

"Mr. President," she said. "It's Angela Tucker."

Deception

"Who likes mashic tricks?" I was still slurring. Miss Ruby and Sean looked at me blankly.

"Card tricks and stuff. I'm a mash-ishcan," I said. I lifted my head again and stared at Miss Ruby with one eye and then the other, like I was still looped on whatever she gave me. In truth, it had almost worn off. This would be my best magic trick ever, if I could convince them I was still whacked out. No pressure.

"Oh, here they are," I said. I picked a deck of cards up off the desk and tried shuffling them, making it look like I had absolutely no hand or eye coordination. They didn't shoot me or anything so I guess they either found me mildly amusing or just confusing. I tried again and this time, as I shuffled, the cards scattered all over the desktop.

"Oopsie," I said. "Tha' no good." I picked up another deck and held it up in front of my eyes, like I needed to study it carefully before it could be used. This time the cards shot out of my hand and flew over the desktop. A few scattered on the floor.

"Oh, no," I said. "I made a mesh." Then I giggled. "Better clean thish up."

"How much of that stuff did you give him again?" Sean asked.

Miss Ruby shrugged. I stood up slowly and pretended to have trouble picking up the cards.

"One . . . two . . ."

"Shut up," Sean said.

"Wanna . . . trying to make shure I get them all," I said, looking at him with one eye. For good measure I wobbled a little as I stood. As far as they were concerned I was helpless.

"Just keep quiet," Sean said. Disgusted, he stalked away from his spot by the desk across the library to the window. He stood sulking, staring outside, apparently not a fan of drug-addled teenagers or magicians.

But it served my purpose. As someone who studied magic, I knew the human eye is hardwired by the brain to follow motion. Unless you're concentrating on something else really hard, your eye is drawn to movement. Part of it is a defense mechanism. Something that moves anywhere in your field of vision, even at a distance, could be a predator or potential enemy. But the instinct works well for magic tricks because a magician creates misdirection and gets the audience to look elsewhere, and that's what allows him or her to pull off the trick.

Miss Ruby's eyes followed Sean all the way across the floor to his spot. While she looked in that direction, I palmed her phone, switched it to vibrate, stuffed it in my pocket, and moved mine to where hers had been. Mine was already set on silent mode. When she looked back at me I was still acting like a heavily drugged kid, preoccupied with straightening up a couple of decks of spilled cards. The only thing was, her phone felt like it weighed a thousand pounds in my pocket. I hoped Angela or Boone or somebody got here quick.

And I hoped Miss Ruby didn't need to make a call.

Calling In the Big Guns

"Angela? Is everything all right?" J. R. Culpepper asked.

"Sir, I . . . things are . . . Boone isn't here. I forgot to memorize his number. They took Q." Everything came rushing out of her.

"Boone is looking for the SUV. What do you mean about Q? Who took him?"

"A big, bossy woman. Giant hair, rings on every finger, earrings the size of sea turtles. Said her name was . . ."

"Ruby Spencer. I know who she is. Boone briefed me. I've been looking into her background. Like most cell members, there isn't much there," the president said. Angela could hear some clicking keys over the phone. "However . . . provided he's still wearing it, Q's watch is showing up at her ranch about thirty-five miles from your present location. Now, tell me what happened."

Angela reported everything as accurately as she could.

"And the guy is still there?"

"Yes, sir. I knocked him out with a camera and Croc went

. . . something is not right about Croc . . . that dog went medieval on the guy and then I clocked him. Oh. I already said that."

The president was chuckling.

"Sir, are you laughing?"

"Yes. Because you remind me so much of your mother."

Angela was flattered but had no time to think about that now.

"What are we going to do about Q? You need to get Boone here and . . ."

"Angela, listen to me. I can't pull Boone off his search for the SUV. There could be thousands of lives at stake. And if I call him, he's going to come and get you to safety and go get Quest. He's the single reason I haven't cleared the city and sent in an entire battalion of Marines to find that truck. No. We need to do this together."

"But . . . sir . . . I . . ." Angela took a breath. "What do you want me to do?"

"Angela, I wish there were another way. And this should not be something for any fifteen-year-old girl to deal with. But you're not just any teenager, are you, Angela? You're Malak Tucker's daughter. You've already proven yourself more than capable. We're going to get Q back."

"But how? He's thirty miles away. I can't even drive! Can't we get Felix or–"

"No, we can't. You are going to run this op, Angela Tucker. The good guys need you right now. You're going to rescue Q. I'm going to tell you how. You can do this!"

"Mr. President, I'm going to need help."

"Have no fear. I've got a couple of people in mind. When you hang up, I want you to take the phone cord and tie up the bad guy. Take his cell phone and put it in your pocket. Make sure he can't get loose. I have somebody on the way to take care of him, but they won't be there for a while. After that, head down to the lobby. Someone will meet you there in exactly ten minutes."

"Who? How will I know who it is?"

"Don't worry. You'll know. Now go."

Angela hung up the phone and did as POTUS instructed.

You've Got to Be Kidding

The elevator door opened and Angela and Croc burst into the lobby. It was a mass of teeming bodies and the noise and chaos were nearly overwhelming. The six banks of elevators had golden doors and they opened every few seconds and disgorged another river of people into the already crowded space. Angela circled the lobby, Croc beside her, not sure who or what she should be looking for. She had been in such a hurry that she hadn't asked the president a whole lot of questions.

Angela looked at her watch. J.R. had said ten minutes. It had been exactly seven minutes since she had left the gunman trussed-up in her room. J.R. said she would know the person. For a dog that mostly slept all the time, Croc was full of energy and when she stopped in the middle of the lobby, he kept trotting toward the front door.

"Croc," she hissed, "where are you going? We have to wait here until . . ."

But Croc didn't listen. He kept right on until the automatic doors opened and he walked outside to the front of the hotel where a long line of guests was waiting for cabs. There was also a large crowd surging into the streets, bypassing the cab lines and walking the few blocks to the concert site.

Croc sat apart from the line of people waiting for a cab. Angela went out and stood beside him, studying everyone she could and wondering what in the world was making the dog act so strangely. She was about to implore Croc to go back inside, when a huge silver Cadillac Escalade screeched to a stop in the valet parking lane. She couldn't say why, but something told her this was her ride. Then the driver emerged and her heart sank.

Dirk Peski motioned her toward him. Angela couldn't believe it. Dirk Peski? The Paparazzi Prince? Angela knew he was an operative working with Ziv. He had been involved in their meeting with her mother at Independence Hall, and somehow he'd gotten himself into the White House. He was always snapping photos of celebrities and he'd been tracking them all across the country. So there must have been something to his story. She was also certain she didn't like him. Not one bit. Really, Mr. President? Dirk Peski? She wanted to scream.

Angela was about to turn away and return to the lobby, but as Croc darted toward the vehicle, Peski ran around and opened the door to the backseat. Croc hopped inside. Reluctantly Angela followed. She stood at the open door.

Dirk was back around the car, climbing into the driver's side.

"Get in!" he shouted.

Croc barked and Angela looked at him, sitting on his

haunches in the backseat. *Traitor,* she thought to herself.

Angela got into the front seat. Dirk put the Escalade in gear and sped out of the valet parking area and onto the street. She quickly buckled her seat belt as he maneuvered through traffic.

"Whoa!" Angela hollered as he accelerated to pass a car, veering quickly back into the lane when a truck coming from the other direction nearly collided with them.

"Where are we going?" she demanded.

"To get Q. It's a place called the Firebrand Ranch. J.R. sent the address to my onboard GPS. It's going to take us about thirty minutes to get there. And we have to hook up with someone else nearby. But Q is there. At least his watch is."

"Somebody else?" Angela said, instantly alarmed. "Who?"

Dirk explained to her about the sheriff and what had happened with Eben and Ziv.

"J.R. checked his background. He is on the phone with him right now, explaining enough to get him to help us."

"How did somebody like you get a car like this?" she asked.

"I'm NOC, just like Boone. Well, nobody's like Boone. But I've been working in the trade for a long time. I also truly am the Paparazzi Prince. It's a good cover and it pays pretty well."

Angela snorted. As far as she was concerned, NOC for Dirk meant Noxious Obnoxious Cretin. And he was right about one thing . . . he was nothing like Boone.

"What?" Dirk asked.

"Nothing." She frowned and crossed her arms, biting her lower lip.

"I know what you're thinking. Paparazzi are bad. But let me tell you. I've been around long enough to know that famous people use the press as much as the press uses them."

He gave the Escalade more gas, swerving into the left lane and zooming around two cars before cutting back into the right-hand lane. Angela closed her eyes.

"Just one thing, Dirk. You just want to use everybody. You don't distinguish between people who are truly artists and could care less about the fame part. Like Blaze and my dad," Angela snapped.

"Everybody has their opinion. Roger and Blaze are talented artists. And they're nice people and good parents. But they're also musicians who make a lot of money and are in the public eye. A certain amount of privacy is given up for that. That's just how it is."

"Hmm," is all Angela said.

"Whatever. Can we discuss the philosophy of a free press another time?"

"I want you to know, I don't trust you," Angela said.

"I know," Dirk replied. "But J.R. does. And so does your grandfather."

"Hmm," Angela said.

Dirk just shrugged and kept driving. Angela looked out the window as the city faded behind them. Before too long they were in open country and Dirk put the gas pedal to the floor. Soon they were blazing down a black ribbon of highway.

"You better not get stopped," Angela warned.

"Don't worry, we've got friends in high places," he said.

Thirty minutes later they reached the outskirts of a small town. Dirk pulled into the Valiant County sheriff's station parking lot. Right near the entrance to the lot stood a large panel truck with Valiant County Animal Control on the side. A man in a Stetson and a tan uniform was leaning on the front fender of a sheriff's patrol car.

"How do we know we can trust him?" Angela said.

"Because POTUS vouches for him. And when J.R. vets someone, you can take it to the bank," Dirk said. "Let's go meet our new partner."

As they exited the Escalade, the man walked over to them and shook their hands. Angela liked his no-nonsense demeanor.

"You must be Mr. Peski and Ms. Tucker," he said. "I'm Sheriff Tom Hackett. I have everything ready to go."

A few minutes later, Angela was in the front seat of the cruiser with Sheriff Hackett while Dirk drove the Animal Control truck behind them.

The sheriff was trying to get information out of her. And it was a real struggle. "I have to say, there're probably ten thousand sheriffs in the entire country who don't ever get a personal call from the president of the United States, and here I am in little Valiant County, Texas, and I get two in the same day. You ever heard of such a thing?" he asked.

Angela could tell the man was nervous. By her count, in the short drive from town to the gate of the Firebrand Ranch he asked her seventeen questions, all of them rhetorical. She knew that law-enforcement personnel were trained to ask questions during interrogations. Asking questions disarmed people. It got them to give up information they might not otherwise reveal. But the sheriff did not know that Angela was wise to this tactic and wasn't going to spill. Still, she wanted him on their side. So far he'd seemed somewhat reluctant.

"Hmm. That is pretty unusual, I guess," she said noncommittally.

"And then for the president to tell me the most prominent citizen in my county is involved in a kidnapping! That's so hard to believe. I mean, if it was a kidnapping I sure can't figure out why the president is sending me, you, and a single CIA guy—who doesn't look anything like a CIA agent, I gotta say—and not the FBI."

"I don't know, Sheriff. I'm sure the president has his reasons," she said.

Angela was saved from further questions by their arrival at the ranch. The cruiser stopped in the driveway a good fifty yards from the house. It was finally dark. The lights from the house and the headlights from the vehicles gave off a kind of spooky glow. As the sheriff approached the mansion, he shone his big flashlight around the ground and trees and bushes along the way as if he were looking for something. Dirk had relayed their cover story to them at the station. A rabid dog was reportedly seen in the area. As sheriff, he had come to personally check it out, to make sure Miss Ruby and her staff were safe. Loyal public servant and all that.

Angela opened her door and crept into the back of the panel van. Dirk had changed into a dark blue jumpsuit that said Valiant County Animal Control on the pocket. He held a catchpole with a loop of rope on the end of it. Croc was ready and waiting. Angela took out a note she had written for Q and stuck it in Croc's collar. Croc shot out the back door and started barking and growling and Dirk followed him out.

"Hey, dog!" he shouted. "Hey!"

At first the sheriff had doubted their rescue plan. Dirk was going to pretend to be an animal-control officer and they were going to turn Croc loose. The sheriff was going to try to distract the people in the house and see if Croc could get inside and get Q out.

The sheriff stopped and returned to the van. He had been dubious about relying on the smelly old dog. But Dirk was insistent.

"Sheriff, we don't have a lot of time or options. We can't go in with guns blazing. They'll kill the boy. You're going to have to trust us. And Angela may be fifteen but she's been in the thick of things for a while now. I'm sure J.R. told you all about her. Now we have to get moving."

The sheriff frowned and looked up toward the house. Angela chimed in, trying to reassure and win him over. "I know what it looks like, Sheriff. But that old dog just took down a bad guy holding me at gunpoint. He's a lot more . . . resourceful . . . than he looks," Angela said.

"What if it don't work?" the sheriff asked.

"If that happens, we'll have to come up with another plan," Dirk said.

"I don't like it," the sheriff said.

"You'll have to get in line," Angela said. "Because no one likes it."

When the sheriff reached the front door, a light came on and Miss Ruby opened it. Dirk slipped away in the darkness. He had quickly briefed everyone on their role at the station. When the door opened, Angela could see them talking, and the sheriff was gesturing and holding his hat in his hands and doing a good job of selling their cover story. If he was following the script, the sheriff was telling Miss Ruby that some of her neighbors had been calling the office about a rabid-dog sighting all day and now they had tracked it back to her ranch. He came out to assist and make sure nothing bad happened. Wanted to let her know he was here in person. Making sure everything was okay, like a good local law-enforcement officer would.

Angela closed her eyes and let out a breath. Thank heavens J.R. had been right. The sheriff and Dirk were up to the task.

Now the rest was up to Croc.

Waiting on the Cavalry

Sean, still dressed like a room-service waiter, was rooted to his spot by the window, like he was waiting for a delivery or something. It made me wonder if someone was on the way here. Someone important. Both of them were acting a little skittish, the way you do when you're expecting trouble or you get sent to the principal's office. Not that I had any personal knowledge of that.

Miss Ruby was bad enough, and the thought of someone higher up than her suddenly appearing was really making me squirm. Malak told Boone that Miss Ruby was number three in importance in the cell. That left only two people higher up the ladder.

I had managed to gather up all the cards and had sat back down at the desk, my head bobbing onto my chest. The library was a big room and Miss Ruby paced a lot and spoke in a low voice. Something about ashes and martyrs, which sounded like a bunch of terrorist mumbo jumbo, and then talk about cents and graphs, which made me think they might be working on an expense account or something.

I tried really hard to concentrate on what they were discussing because I knew it could be important. But I wasn't as smart as Angela about this stuff. A few seconds later their conversation grew a little more animated and they began to argue.

"If you think you've got a better idea, why don't you call and ask him?" she said. "In fact, I'll call him right now and you can ask him yourself. Then we'll see how Number One likes being bothered by one of his foot soldiers."

I sat up straighter and tensed. She'd said call *him*. Now I knew that Number One was a man.

Miss Ruby patted all of her pockets. Like someone does when they are trying to find their lighter or their phone. The phone that was currently in *my* pocket. Everything slowed down and I got tunnel vision as Miss Ruby marched toward the desk. I had been caught off-guard and had no time to switch the phone back. This wasn't going to end well. For me.

Miss Ruby stomped across the floor in her fancy cowboy boots. Her eyes roamed over the desk and she spotted "her" phone. As her hand reached for it, I felt like time froze in place.

Outside a dog started barking.

Rescue Dog

Miss Ruby turned around and went back to the window. Sean was peering out into the darkness. Neither of them appeared overly concerned. Robert stood still in the middle of the room, watching me. Very still. Like a statue. I really wanted to stand up and get ready to run, but was afraid Sean and his itchy trigger finger would not appreciate it. Besides, Robert also looked like he could squish me like a bug. Croc was here. Which didn't necessarily mean that Angela was, but I preferred not to think about that. I doubted Croc would have left Angela alone with a gunman. Most of the drug had worn off. I just had to remember to make them think I was still under the influence of it. But now I had a pounding headache and my mouth was really dry.

"You two check this out," Miss Ruby said. "We had that rabid dog here earlier today, maybe it's back."

A rabid dog? I remember Boone saying something about Croc acting like a mad dog while he got inside the house. I just wondered what I was supposed to do, seeing that I was still sitting in a room full of terrorists.

Sean and Robert left the room. Miss Ruby stayed at the window. I eyed my phone that was lying on the desk in place of hers and toyed with the idea of switching it back. But if I could get out of here, there could be a ton of intelligence on her phone. Even direct contacts to the highest leadership of the ghost cell. I had to find a way to hang on to it.

There was a lot of shouting and noise going on outside. The barking, growling, and snapping grew louder. It sounded like a mini riot.

Sean and Robert had left the library door open. And now somebody was knocking on the front door.

Miss Ruby cursed. Apparently there was no one else in the house to answer the door. The knocking continued.

"Oh, for goodness' sake," she muttered. She headed for the door but not before turning to give me a warning. "You best . . ." She stopped, because I was slumped back in the chair, my eyes closed and my body limp. I wanted her to think I'd been fighting the drug as hard as I could, but finally couldn't hold out any more.

When we were in Kitty Hawk, Malak had told us Bethany had pretended to be unconscious using something called yoga breath. I didn't know how to do that, but I tried to make my breathing deep and slow. I willed my heart to beat slower but wasn't sure that would happen.

She was getting closer and I forced myself to stay still. A few moments later her fingertips touched my neck, checking my pulse. She snapped her fingers next to my face a couple of times and I managed not to flinch. After that she shook me by the arm. I let out the best fake snore of my life.

Miss Ruby seemed satisfied because I heard her striding across the library floor and the door creaked slightly as she pushed it farther open. I waited another three seconds before I cracked open an eye. She was gone. I counted to ten to make sure she didn't pop back in to try and catch me faking her out, but she didn't. Still, there was very little time.

I stood up. I jammed all my stuff into my pockets and hustled over to the window. It was locked and with no way to open it that I could see. It was dark outside. The library was off to the side of the house and from the angle of this window I couldn't see the front door, just part of the side yard and the faint outline of the road and fence off in the distance. Though my field of vision was limited, I could hear the noise and commotion outside. Miss Ruby had gone to the front door, but maybe there was a back entrance. But Sean and Robert were who knows where—outside or inside—and I didn't especially want to run into them. It was a huge house and it had to have more than a couple of ways in and out.

I envied Boone. I'd been trying his little illusion but I still hadn't figured it out. Now would have been the perfect time to use it.

Poof! There He Is

I was almost to the library door when I nearly tripped over Croc who had just *poofed* into the room. Though it startled me, I couldn't believe how happy I was to see that old smelly dog.

"Croc!" I whispered.

Miss Ruby was talking to somebody at the front door. Now I wasn't sure what to do. Croc bent his head around at the neck and I spied a piece of paper stuffed into his collar.

Q,

Croc is going to create a diversion. Get out of the house somehow and head for the van parked behind the sheriff's cruiser. Try not to let anyone see you. The sheriff is on our side.

Angela

"Get out of the house somehow?" I whispered to myself. "Thanks for the specific instructions, sis!"

"Okay," I said quietly, "let's figure a way out of here." I looked down, but Croc was gone.

Not more than three seconds later, barking and growling

and shouting came from outside. When I peered out the door of the library, I could see Miss Ruby down the hall, standing at the front door. She was talking to the sheriff, who Angela insisted was on our side. All I had seen of the house when they first brought me here was the front door, foyer, hallway, and the library. If there was another way out, I didn't have much time to find it.

The sheriff was looking over Miss Ruby's shoulder and must have seen me, but he didn't let his face betray anything. Instead he said, "It sounds like that mutt is a little hard to handle. I better see if they need some help. I just wanted you to know I was taking care of this personally, Miss Ruby."

I had no idea what she would do next. So I darted silently out of the library and into the bathroom across the hall. I kept the door open slightly so I could see the front door. My unconscious act must have convinced her because she walked past the library toward the back of the house. When she was out of sight I hustled down the hall to the front door and opened it a crack.

The lights by the front door cut into the darkness a little. I heard more barking and shouting coming from the rear of the house. Croc had led everyone, including Miss Ruby, to the back so I could make it to the van. What a dog. As I ran, someone shouted, "There it is!" followed by "Grab it, you idiot!" They didn't know they had very little chance of catching Croc if he didn't want to be caught.

The van was parked right behind the sheriff's car. It wasn't that far, but it seemed like miles. I ran as fast as I could to the rear door and threw it open. When I jumped in, there was

Angela, waiting. I was never so glad to see someone in my entire life.

"Oh, wow!" we both said at the same time.

"Thank God you're okay, I thought . . ." I started to say but couldn't finish. Angela just nodded, a little teary-eyed. I gave her a huge hug.

"If you hadn't come out in another minute, we figured you might be unconscious or too drugged to escape," Angela said. "I was going to try to sneak in and find you."

"For some weird reason, those drugs didn't work on me. I have a really bad headache and a dry mouth, but I faked them into thinking I was looped," I said.

Angela filled me in on how she'd knocked out the guy in the hotel room with Croc's help. While she was talking I made a mental note never to get Angela really mad at me.

I showed her Miss Ruby's iPhone and told her how I'd gotten it.

"That's great, Q!" she said.

"It's great when we get away. I need to call X-Ray right now. He has to copy it or clone it or whatever he does. What is his number?" I asked.

Angela stared at me, a blank look on her face. "I don't know it. The gunman forced me to smash my phone and I never memorized everyone's numbers. They were all preprogrammed," she said.

"Oh, boy. I hope we get out of here before they find out I've got it," I said.

Just then the back door to the van opened and there was Dirk Peski, holding a wiggling Croc on the end of a catchpole.

Croc was lunging and snarling and snapping at Dirk and in the glow from the van's taillights, Dirk looked a little petrified. We knew that Croc was putting on a show. However, it appeared that Boone's faithful companion was no fan of the Paparazzi Prince either. Dirk slammed the back door shut, no doubt relieved to have a steel barrier between him and the mutt. Outside we heard the sheriff telling Miss Ruby he was sorry for the inconvenience and was happy the "rabid" dog was no longer a threat.

Dirk opened the driver's door and hopped in.

"Dirk Peski?" I said to Angela. I couldn't believe it. Dirk?

Angela shrugged. "According to him, he doesn't just help Ziv, he's also NOC. I had to call the president. He sent Dirk," she said.

"The president? Of the United States? Our president? J. R. Culpepper sent Dirk Peski?" I was stunned.

"Hey!" Dirk said in mock indignation.

Huh, I thought. Dirk, of all people. This was the trouble with all of this spy stuff, as I saw it: You never knew who to trust.

"Dirk, do you have X-Ray's phone number?" I asked.

"Yes," he said as he backed the van into a turnaround and steered it down the driveway toward the road.

I waited.

"Would you mind giving it to me, Dirk?"

He recited the number and I called X-Ray. Like always, he picked up before the phone even rang.

"X-Ray, it's Q, is Boone there?" I asked.

"No, he's working the crowd right now," he answered.

"Okay, can you do some of your tech stuff with the phone I'm calling from? Keep what's on here because it might be valuable to Malak." I explained what I'd done, and how Miss Ruby needed to think my phone was hers.

"Yes, I can do that. What's the serial number of the phone you have?" he asked. I recited it to him.

"Give me ten minutes," he said.

"We might not even have three minutes, X-Ray," I said.

"I'll do what I can," he replied and hung up the phone.

The driveway had a little circle in it near the house and we pulled around it and down the drive to the road. We turned right and sped away. About five minutes later my phone rang; it was X-Ray.

"The SIM cards on both phones have been overridden. Unless she's memorized her serial number, she's going to think your phone is hers. But I managed to save all of the data that was on her phone. We'll be able to mine it once you get it to me. I just spoke to Boone. He says you guys are to stay at the sheriff's station until this is over."

I was silent a minute. Boone didn't want us back there. I understood why. And I doubted that if the sheriff knew everything, he'd take two kids into a city that might have a huge explosion at any minute.

"Q? Did you hear me? Boone says stay there," X-Ray said.

"Yes. I got it. Okay." X-Ray, like always, hung up without saying goodbye. But I kept the phone to my ear.

"Yes. What do you need me to do?" I said. I was going to lie and I didn't feel good about it but I knew Angela would understand and hopefully Dirk and the sheriff would buy it.

"We'll do our best to get it to you," I said. I winked at Angela. She would probably guess Boone would want us to stay someplace safe until this was over. But she was also smart and would play along.

My mom and Angela's dad and a bunch of other people I cared about were right in the middle of a potential blast zone. We just might be the extra sets of eyes that saw the bad guys and stopped this whole thing. I had to try.

"Got it," I said into the dead phone (and for Dirk's benefit). "We'll get it there as fast as we can. I'll tell the sheriff." Now I pretended to hang up.

"What's going on?" Dirk asked.

"We need to get this phone to X-Ray. When he was doing the switch on the phone, he found some app or something on her phone that might be a kill switch. It needs a code to open it. If he has the actual phone he might be able to crack the encryption." I lied like I have never lied in my life. Even Angela cocked her head at me.

Dirk was looking at me in the rearview and I held his gaze. I am a magician. Or at least I hoped I was right at that moment. Deception.

"Okay," he said. We were a couple of miles from the ranch.

The van slowed and pulled over and the sheriff's car stopped behind us.

All of us got out, including Croc. The sheriff looked me over.

"You all right, son?" he asked.

"Yes, sir," I said.

"Is anybody ever going to tell me what's going on here?"

he asked.

"No time right now, Sheriff," Dirk said. "But Boone's tech guy has determined Miss Ruby's phone has got some really valuable intel on it. He needs it ASAP. And you need to get Angela and Q back right away, before their parents find out they're missing. We're talking lights and sirens here, Sheriff. Can you do that?"

Even though Dirk thought he was telling the truth, I marveled at how convincing he could be. Maybe being the Paparazzi Prince was good training for being a spy.

"Somebody owes me an explan–"

"It's probably best that you don't know," Dirk interrupted. "We have no idea how many people Miss Ruby has here. If they find out you're involved . . ."

"That's what everybody keeps telling me," Sheriff Hackett said. "Can't say as that makes me real happy."

"Sheriff, if we could tell you, we would," I said. "But right now this phone has got information Boone needs and we need to get it to him as fast as we can. It's a matter of life and death," I said, holding the phone up in my hand and waving it around. I looked at Angela and she raised her eyebrows at me. I wanted to wait until the last possible moment to tell the sheriff about the car bomb. If he found out, I was pretty sure he'd refuse to take us.

He looked at me. I was a horrible liar and I got the feeling he knew I wasn't being truthful. But Angela had told me in the van about calling J.R. and how he'd called the sheriff twice today. So he was probably not going to want to do anything that might make the most powerful man in the world upset.

There were several seconds of silence. Finally Dirk jumped in and pushed him a little more.

"Right now I need you to take Angela and Q back to San Antonio. I'm sure once you get there, Boone will give you all the information he can. I'll take the van back to your station and get my Escalade. We need to hurry. They'll know Q is gone soon and they'll come looking. The kids will be safer with Boone."

"Why don't you take them?" the sheriff asked Dirk.

"Because you have a police car. You can get them through the crowds and other places where I'll get bottled up. You've got to do this, Sheriff," Dirk said.

"What are you going to do?" the sheriff asked Dirk.

"What I do best. I'll be watching your back," Dirk said as he climbed back into the Animal Control van and sped away. Angela, Croc, and I got into the backseat of the cruiser and the sheriff headed for San Antonio.

I tried not to think about anything but the fact that we were traveling toward a city where a massive car bomb was looking for a target.

And I hoped like heck that Boone could figure out a way to stop it.

Now You See Him

Miss Ruby returned to the library to find Q nowhere in sight. She hustled across the room and looked under the desk. He was gone. No matter. He had nowhere to go. Her nearest neighbor was six miles away. The ranch was massive but they'd find him.

"Robert! Sean! Get in here!" she shouted, not needing the intercom this time.

"What? You left him alone?" Sean said when Miss Ruby told them what happened.

"You saw him. He's full of drugs. When I left him he was passed out cold in the chair and I know because I checked him. He's probably in the house some–"

She stopped speaking, spying a playing card that had fallen off the desk and now lay propped on its side on the carpeted floor, tilted against the wooden desk.

"Wait a minute," she said, snatching the card up off the floor. Turning it over revealed the ace of spades.

As she paced back and forth thinking, she grabbed her

cigarette case off the desk. Smoking–filthy habit that it was–helped her think. The pack inside was empty and as she removed it, a tiny round piece of metal tumbled out of it and bounced on the floor. Picking it up and turning it over in her fingers, she found it resembled a very small hearing-aid battery.

"What is that?" Robert asked.

"I don't know," she said. "Way too small to have a transmitter so it's probably not a bug. Maybe a tracking device?"

"Tracking device?" Sean said. "Why would . . . do you suppose the kid had it on him?"

"Maybe." She paused a moment to consider it. "Let's think about it. Ariel and the others snatched them at Kitty Hawk. Maybe whoever is watching them upped their security." She tossed the tiny device to Sean, who examined it closely.

"The rabid dog. Dang it. The sheriff didn't come here for the rabid dog, it was a setup. . . . He came to get the kid out without us knowing. We already reported a rabid dog once today. There would be a record of that. I'll bet you a thousand dollars he brought another dog from the pound. Let it act up outside. Bingo, perfect cover story."

Miss Ruby pounded her clenched right fist into the open palm of her left hand. "Somebody is onto us."

"Hold on," Robert said. "Let's not panic. The sheriff is a dope. How would he . . . ?"

"Maybe he is, maybe he isn't. But he probably had help from whoever is watching those kids. Remember Ariel and her crew had the boy and his sister cold. Ariel don't make mistakes, sugar. Whoever is watching them got them back. We're dealing with someone smart. I think that kid was playing us." Miss Ruby paused and picked up the playing card. "Like a magician."

"But you shot him full of . . ." Sean said.

"He faked me out," she said. "Sometimes those drugs don't work. People can have a tolerance for them or they need a bigger dose to knock them out, even a kid. Read a book once in a while."

"What are we going to do?" Sean asked.

Miss Ruby picked up her phone from the desk. She called the sheriff's office.

"Hi, sugar, this is Miss Ruby Spencer. Oh no, honey. It's not an emergency, honey pie. But I was wonderin' if y'all could put me in touch with the sheriff. I see. Uh-huh. Thank you, darlin'." She ended the call.

"The sheriff isn't in. He hasn't called in a while. My guess is he's on his way back to San Antonio with that snot-nosed kid."

"What do we do?" Robert asked.

"We've got to go grab him and get out of here. Trust me on this, boys. If Number One finds out about this, we're all dead anyway."

Miss Ruby pushed another button and held the phone to her ear. After a few seconds she disconnected the call.

"Marco's phone is going to voice mail. He should be on his way back now. If he killed the girl and left, like he should have, he knows he's supposed to answer his phone."

"Maybe his phone died or the towers are overloaded.

There's a ton of people in San Antonio for that concert," Robert said.

"Maybe. But what if she had the same kind of tracking signal on her?" she said. "Look at how small that thing is. What if someone came and got the girl out and then . . ."

"Killing a sheriff is going to bring heat. And what is so special about the kid, anyway?" Robert asked.

"Tell me something I don't know. But if we don't get him back, a dead sheriff will be the least of your worries. The others aren't going to be happy if we fail again. Believe me. Let's go."

In the corner of the library was a large wooden armoire. Ruby opened the doors to reveal a metal gun safe built into the wall. She entered the combination and the door popped open. There was a rack full of M-4 automatic rifles inside. Sean and Robert each took one and she grabbed one for herself.

While they checked the loads in their weapons, Miss Ruby grabbed a few extra clips of ammunition and handed them to each man. Stuffing the ammo into their pockets they headed out of the library and through the front door.

Miss Ruby tried not to show her concern. She'd spent years working her way up to the Five. She didn't want to lose her place in one night because of a stupid kid. People who failed the ghost cell didn't live very long.

She tried thinking of a way out of this if they failed to get Quest Munoz back. And she couldn't.

Outside they climbed into their black Suburban and sped off into the night.

Quality Time

Ziv and Eben sat in their nondescript brown Toyota Corolla on a side street on the South Side of Chicago, not far from U.S. Cellular Field. It was lined on both sides with parked cars and they blended in nicely. After they arrived in Chicago, Agent Callaghan contacted them with Malak Tucker's location. Callaghan watched over her until they arrived. When they notified him they were in position, he drove away and returned to the hotel to sleep.

So far there had been no movement from Malak. She remained in the house as instructed. Ziv had no doubt she was nearly stir-crazy.

Eben was looking at his watch and making sure Ziv noticed. "It really is a stunning timepiece," he said.

"As I have heard the first three hundred times you've said it," Ziv groused. "It is not like it is a Rolex."

"A Rolex is cliché," Eben said. "Not everyone has an Omega Seamaster, personally presented to them by the president of the United States."

"The president of the United States didn't present it to you personally," Ziv said. "It was handed to you by one of his flunkies."

"Not a flunky, a U.S. Secret Service agent," Eben reminded him.

"Yes, yes. Beautiful watch. You are so lucky. You are also making me nauseous. We are on a stakeout. I like my stakeouts to be quiet," Ziv said. He flipped on the radio. The White Sox were playing a home game and off in the distance they could see the lights of U.S. Cellular Field, a bright and stunning beacon in the dark night.

"You are a fan of American baseball?" Eben asked, skeptical.

"I have come to appreciate it to a certain degree, though I am by no means an expert. I've found listening to baseball on the radio relaxes me and helps keep me focused," Ziv said.

"You never cease to amaze me, Ziv. Who would have thought? We should be enemies. In the old days we would be trying to kill each other and now we are on the same side," Eben said.

"Times change. People change. And I am on no *other side* but that of my daughter and granddaughter. Their safety is now all I care about. In fact . . ." The chirping of his phone interrupted him and he snapped it open. "Hello," he said.

Ziv listened to the caller, asking a few pointed questions. Eben sat up in the passenger seat. When Ziv disconnected the call, Eben waited expectantly for the old man to speak.

"That was Dirk. The ghost cell took Q from his hotel tonight and kept him at the Firebrand Ranch. Dirk and the sheriff were able to retrieve him, with Angela's help. Angela managed to escape a gunman who was holding her at the hotel. Now they are en route back to San Antonio with the sheriff. Dirk will be watching their tail."

"Angela . . ." Eben unconsciously rubbed his jaw where Angela had loosened a few of his teeth with a well-timed and effective kick. "She is a remarkable young woman. You should be very proud. Shall we inform Malak of this news?"

Ziv thought a moment, then shook his head. "No. You are correct. Angela is much like her mother. And in some ways a great deal like her aunt Anmar. But if we tell Malak that Angela is in danger, neither you nor I or any power on earth will be able to keep her here. No. We wait until we know Angela is safe before we tell Malak. Otherwise . . ."

"Otherwise what?" Eben asked, but he knew the answer already.

"Otherwise the Leopard will go on the hunt."

"You are right," Eben said, making a show of looking at his watch. "Now is not the time."

Ziv groaned and slumped in his seat.

The Second Monkey

Dirk Peski walked across the sheriff's parking lot to his Escalade. His conversation with Ziv had been brief and he knew the old man was worried. It had only been about four years since he had learned of Malak's existence. Now his granddaughter, Angela, was in harm's way and Dirk understood how powerless he felt.

He decided to go past the ranch and gather a little bit more intel before he returned to San Antonio. This Miss Ruby woman would discover very quickly that Q was gone, and Dirk wanted to do some on-site recon. Q and Angela were probably fine now, as it was unlikely Miss Ruby would chance a second kidnapping attempt.

But if he had learned anything, it was that you could never be too safe.

With the sky overcast and no stars or moonlight showing through, the darkness in this wide-open countryside seemed absolute. The occasional house or ranch provided some light but the headlights on the Escalade seemed inefficient in the gloom.

Dirk slowed the car as the house came into view. The lights were still on inside. But as he drew nearer, he was startled when a black Suburban, running with its lights off, appeared out of the darkness. It roared past him, heading in the opposite direction.

Caution was required. If someone in the Suburban was watching him in the rearview mirror and observed him hitting the brakes, it might alert them that someone was onto them. Waiting until the shadow of the Suburban faded into the darkness, he flipped off his lights and braked. His tires squealing on the asphalt, he spun the wheel hard to the left. The rear end of the vehicle spun to the right and the car did a one-eighty turn. His tires smoked as they bit into the road, and he gave the Escalade gas. A few miles ahead this road would reach the county highway leading to San Antonio. He couldn't be sure, but off in the distance he thought he saw a set of taillights, but they blinked out of sight as the road rose and dipped.

That was the most direct route back to the city and if the sheriff was up ahead with Miss Ruby on his tail, he hoped he could get there in time. The pavement was long, flat, and black. He again thought he spied a set of taillights, and offered up a silent prayer that it was the sheriff's car. But without warning, cutting through the dark night, high beams suddenly burst to life, followed by staccato bursts of light that could only be automatic-weapons fire.

Dirk punched it.

Attacked

I tried to will the sheriff to go faster. It didn't work. I tried *poofing*, like Boone. No good.

"Do you suppose all this is true, what the president told me, about terrorists and all that?" the sheriff asked. He was still using the "ask a question to try to get 'em talking" technique. Sheriff Hackett had yet to figure out he was no match for Angela.

"I don't know why the president would lie about something like that," Angela said. "After all, Sheriff, they were holding Q, weren't they? And by the way, do you think we could pick up the pace?" she said. As if to emphasize the urgency, Croc barked from the backseat where he sat on his haunches between us. The sheriff gave the car more gas.

"I reckon they are what the president says they are. Still, this just sounds like something out of a Hollywood movie," he muttered.

"Believe me, Sheriff," Angela muttered. "Movies don't even come close."

"I suppose. You seem to know a lot about this stuff, miss. How is that, if you don't mind my asking?"

"My mother is . . . was . . . a U.S. Secret Service agent," Angela said quietly.

"Was?" the sheriff asked, looking at us in the rearview mirror. Angela stared out the window into the dark.

"She died in the line of duty," I said. Even though the president had recruited the sheriff, I'd learned that Boone believed in the need-to-know doctrine. And the fewer people who knew that Malak Tucker was really alive, the better.

"Oh. I'm sorry. I didn't . . . I had . . ." the sheriff was at a loss for words.

But not for long.

"What do you suppose is the story with this Dirk fella?" he asked. "The president said he—"

Without warning the interior of the car was filled with blinding light. A huge SUV had emerged from the darkness and then hit the brights from only a few yards behind us.

"Gun it, Sheriff!" Angela shouted.

The rear window exploded in a hail of automatic-weapons fire.

A Bit of a Pickle

Glass flew everywhere. The noise from the guns was overwhelming. Croc barked and growled. I'm pretty sure I was screaming as the car was swerving back and forth. The seat belts kept us strapped in place and Angela and I both grabbed hold of Croc but it still felt a little like we were on an amusement park ride.

"Holy–!" the sheriff shouted, jerking the wheel to the left to get out of the line of fire. The Suburban immediately followed and the gunshots started again. I could hear bullets thumping into metal and sparks flew all around us.

"Stay down!" the sheriff hollered. It was hard for us to get very far down below the rear window with our seat belts holding us in place. It was a tough choice. If we stayed belted in, we were probably going to get shot. But if we undid them and climbed down on the floor, we could be injured in a crash. Angela and I reached the same conclusion–we'd rather not get shot–and released our seat belts and rolled onto the floor. I just hoped the sheet metal of the car could stand up to the onslaught.

"If you've got a phone, get on it and call for help! The radio just took a bullet," the sheriff shouted.

"Q! Can you do it?" Angela shouted. She was holding on to Croc with all her might, trying to keep him from flopping around in the backseat. Broken glass was everywhere and if we weren't careful we were going to cut ourselves to ribbons.

"Hold on!" the sheriff shouted.

The Suburban's headlights got suddenly brighter because the vehicle rammed into the rear of the cruiser and we were flung head first into the back of the front seat. It hurt. All the while I was scrambling to reach the phone and just as I cleared it from my pocket the Suburban rammed us again and it was jolted from my hand. It skittered away under the seat and out of reach.

"Go faster!" Angela screamed.

The noise was deafening and I was pretty sure this was it. We'd run out of time and luck. I just hoped that Boone would be able to find the SUV and stop the bomb before anyone else got hurt.

But lucky for us, Sheriff Hackett had a trick or two up his sleeve. The cruiser was a powerful, heavy vehicle lined with thick steel. It was also capable of great speed. We felt the car accelerate and the gunfire stopped momentarily as we swerved back and forth and pulled ahead of the Suburban, leaving Miss Ruby and her henchmen unable to get off an accurate shot.

I tried reaching for the phone but couldn't find it in the darkness with the car swerving all over the place. The interior of the car grew brighter again as the Suburban gained on us. When they were right on our tail, the sheriff cut the wheel to the left into the other lane and hit the brakes. The big SUV shot past us as the cruiser screeched to a halt. The SUV's tires bit hard into the pavement and the driver must have had to struggle to keep it from rolling over. I peeked my head up over the seat to find the windshield a spider web of cracks. The sheriff was grabbing his shotgun from the gun rack attached to the dash.

The sheriff racked the shotgun and was about to open the door when, out of nowhere, Dirk Peski's Escalade shot into view. It slowed just slightly as it pulled past the cruiser, then accelerated, hitting the Suburban broadside. Dirk's vehicle pushed the Suburban along the pavement, its wheels churning black smoke. Keeping his foot on the gas, he shoved the Suburban another thirty yards down the road. It collided with a bridge overpass.

"Stay here!" the sheriff yelled. He left the car and ran toward the wreck, holding the shotgun at port arms. Reaching the driver's door of the Escalade, he yanked it open and pulled Dirk free. Dirk looked a little rattled and the sheriff looped Dirk's arm over his shoulder and hustled him away from the smoking mass of twisted metal.

"Get down!" the sheriff shouted. Angela and I ducked down in the backseat just as the gas tanks of the Escalade and the SUV caught fire and exploded in a massive fireball.

Counting Down

"Uly, what have you got? I need a status report!" Boone said over the Bluetooth. He was near the rear of the crowd that had piled into the plaza and he could see the Alamo behind the stage. While he waited, he kept scanning for any sign of the terrorists. There was silence on the line as everyone waited for Uly to respond.

"Uly? Copy?" Boone asked again.

"Sorry. I think I've got eyes on one of the guys but I can't tell. He's wearing glasses and a different hat. And it's dark. I'm sending a photo to X-Ray now for confirmation," Uly said.

"Okay," Boone said. "Keep him in sight while X-Ray runs it."

"Copy," Uly said.

X-Ray's fingers flew over the keyboard as the picture appeared on his screen. The screen flickered and blinked as it compared the photo to the four from the warehouse. Boone waited and a few seconds later X-Ray's voice said, "Negative. It's not a match."

"Negative, Uly," Boone said.

"Copy that," Uly said.

Boone strolled along, weaving in and out of the mass of people, looking for anyone matching the description.

"Felix," he said. "Have you got anything?"

"Negative. I've had my binoculars on every white SUV I've seen and I've yet to spot a Tahoe. I've seen Fords, Toyotas, Chryslers, and a Hyundai, but not a single Chevy. I think it must be a state law that you have to own a white SUV to live in Texas. But I haven't seen one that looks suspicious yet. Nobody making any circles around the plaza or anything," Felix said.

"Copy that. Stay alert. Holler if you see anything that's at all weird," Boone said. "Vanessa, what's your location?"

"I checked out the parking garage across from the plaza. No Tahoe there either. I'm working the crowd now, but I haven't noticed anyone yet that matches our perps," she said.

"All right, copy," Boone said, his voice full of discouragement.

"What am I missing, X-Ray?" he asked.

X-Ray was silent. He knew Boone was asking a rhetorical question and didn't really want an answer. He'd worked enough ops with Boone to know he sometimes got like this.

"Maybe it isn't the concert," Boone said. "Maybe it's some other target."

"That would go completely against their SOP," X-Ray said. And Boone had to agree with X-Ray. Choosing another target would be completely against their standard operating procedure. It wasn't easy to make a car bomb. In the movies they popped up everywhere, but in real life it was difficult to gather the explosives needed to do enough damage. It would be a hollow gesture for the cell to destroy something without also killing a lot of people, or at least a few important people. They would use the vehicle in a way that would inflict the greatest number of casualties. And in San Antonio tonight that meant the concert. But what if it were something else? Boone was always willing to consider he might have missed something.

"X-Ray, aside from the concert and the Alamo itself, what other targets are there in San Antonio? The top five things the ghost cell could take out and score a major propaganda victory?"

There was no reply for a few seconds and Boone envisioned X-Ray with his fingers flying over the keyboards in the van as he researched possibilities.

"There's an air force base nearby," X-Ray said. "San Antonio is the regional banking center for southwest Texas. There's the historical significance of the Alamo. If someone were to blow up or damage that old mission with a bomb, we wouldn't need a military response. Every Texan in the state with a pickup truck and a shotgun would chase them to the gates of, well . . . someplace really hot," he said. "Fort Hood is a major military deployment center but that's three and a half hours from here. I gotta say, Boone, if I had to pick, it would be the concert and/or the Alamo itself. The most potential for death and destruction, the highest degree of symbolism, and the easiest to breach in terms of security."

Boone thought X-Ray was probably right; he had learned

to trust his team. It didn't hurt to make sure he wasn't missing something. So far they had yet to see any of the suspects, and that fact ate at him, making him doubt his instincts.

He was about to order Uly and Vanessa back to the perimeter when Vanessa cut in over the Bluetooth.

"I think I've got something," she said. "Maneuvering for a photo now. Stand by."

They waited silently for the image to show up on X-Ray's computer screen. Finally the picture appeared and X-Ray ran it against the suspect photos. A few seconds later everyone heard him say, "It's a match."

"Vanessa, we have confirmation that's one of the men. Move in and keep him in sight. See if he hooks up with any of the others. But if you think he's going to use something like a detonator, or use a phone, take him out. Uly, you move toward her position. Vanessa, give Felix your location. Felix, see if you can pick them up through your scope. We might need you. Stay ready."

The chatter between the SOS agents went back and forth on the line.

"Where are you, Boone?" Vanessa asked.

"Don't worry," he said. "I'm around."

Monkey Shines

When the noise of the explosion passed, we looked up from behind the backseat. The sheriff slowly stood up and helped Dirk to his feet. Dirk's arm was hanging by his side, as if it were broken. Angela, Croc, and I sat up in the backseat, our ears still ringing from the noise. We were covered in broken glass. The good news was that so much adrenaline had pumped through me in the last few minutes, I felt no lingering effects of the drug.

"Are you all right?" I asked Angela.

"I'm okay," she said. "Although I'd really prefer not to go through that again. Ever. If it's all the same." We carefully picked our way out of the car, trying to avoid getting cut or scratched. We were going to have to come up with a whopper to explain the way we looked. I had a scratch on the back of my hand and Angela's cheek was bleeding.

"Me either. We'd better check on Dirk and the sheriff," I said. I wondered how the sheriff was going to explain this to . . . whomever sheriffs explained things to. The car was so full of bullet holes it looked like a sponge.

"Are you okay, Dirk?" I asked. His face looked a little pale, like maybe he was going into shock. The sheriff was beside himself with anger.

"All right. I've had enough innuendo and half-truths to last me a lifetime. Somebody better tell me everything right now!" The sheriff was beyond his boiling point.

Dirk took out his phone. "What happened is, there has been a horrible accident. Three Valiant County citizens were killed in a collision with Dirk Peski, the Paparazzi Prince, who may or may not have been intoxicated. I'm going to call 9-1-1 and you are going to deliver Angela and Q back to Boone in San Antonio. As quickly as you can."

The sheriff reached out to stop Dirk.

"Are you insane? You can't call 9-1-1. You'll go to jail. Especially if you take the blame."

"Don't worry about me, Sheriff," Dirk said. "As I think you know, I've got friends in high places. I won't be in jail for long. There will be an investigation, I'll spend a few days, maybe a couple of weeks at most, in the clink. Then I'll be found to be not at fault for the accident and sent on my way. The Valiant County sheriff will warn me not to show my face around these parts again. This is how it works."

"I don't understand any of this," the sheriff said.

"Sheriff Hackett, you're a good man. And I'm sorry you got caught up in this. I truly am. But there are many lives at stake. And I've already said too much. I need you to see this through. Get Angela and Q to San Antonio. Hand them over to Boone. I'm going to make that 9-1-1 call. Then I'm probably going to sit down on the ground and pass out because my arm is killing me. But I need to know you'll do what I ask."

I decided then that maybe Dirk Peski wasn't such a bad guy after all.

"All right, all right, call it in," the sheriff said, "but when I get back to the station—"

"When you get back to the station, you and I are never going to speak of this night again, right?" Dirk asked.

The sheriff frowned. I admit I felt a little sorry for him. But I was also glad he was on our side. After all, he'd just saved our lives.

The sheriff helped us clear most of the broken glass out of the backseat. Angela, Croc, and I climbed in. As we pulled away, we heard Dirk saying into his phone, "Hello! My name is Dirk Peski. I think I just caused an accident out here on County Road 19. You'd better send fire trucks and ambulances . . ."

The rest of his words were lost as we zoomed away into the darkness.

Crowd Control

The crowd was enormous and the SOS team was moving in on its first target. Despite her small stature, Vanessa managed to make her way through the masses without being jostled or bumped. She liked to tell the team that her reflexes were razor sharp "for an old broad." This usually caused all of them, even Felix and Uly, to laugh nervously, for Vanessa was quite deadly. Boone also said she had an uncanny ability to read people, often referring to her as "the human lie detector."

But another skill she possessed was her tracking ability. With her white hair, lined face, and nonthreatening demeanor, she was invisible to almost everyone. Especially her targets. Until it was too late for them. Once she latched on to someone, they had to be as good at shaking a tail as she was at following them. There weren't very many people in the world that good.

The guy was about twenty yards ahead of her. She was glad X-Ray was able to confirm his identity. It made her completely comfortable using any means necessary to deal with him. Vanessa had done a lot of dangerous things in her time, but she considered terrorists the worst kinds of cowards. She had no regrets about taking this guy out.

She couldn't yet see Uly over the crush of the gathering audience. Tracking a suspect in a crowd this size was difficult and dangerous. It required staying close enough that they didn't get lost among all the people, but not so near they sensed your presence.

Vanessa always kept her wardrobe flexible, usually wearing a windbreaker tied around her waist or a sweater around her shoulders. She would keep a couple of collapsible hats in her pockets along with some scarves and sunglasses. It allowed her to quickly alter her appearance, making it more difficult for her targets to realize they were being followed.

Vanessa was reasonably sure the suspect was not giving her any thought at all. Off to her left she finally spotted Uly, who held his phone to his ear to disguise the fact that he was on the prowl. Normally Boone wouldn't send Uly or Felix into a crowd like this because they were so easily noticed. But he didn't have any choice.

Vanessa shortened the distance between her and the suspect when she saw him reach into his pocket.

Moving quickly, she closed on him. With his back to her, Vanessa twisted at the waist and drove her fist into his kidney. The sudden shocking pain caused him to straighten up and throw his head and shoulders back. Before he could cry out or react to the pain, she drove her thumb hard into the large nerve bundle below his left ear. The blow staggered the man and rendered him temporarily paralyzed.

Uly suddenly appeared and, acting as if he were the

suspect's drunken friend, hooked his arm around the man's neck and said loudly, "Dude, you've got to slow down, the party's gonna last all night." Vanessa had already veered away, swallowed up by the mass of people. And to the passersby, the two men appeared to be a couple of wasted partiers. In fact Uly was squeezing off the man's air supply until he lapsed completely into unconsciousness. "Whoa. We gotta find you a seat, bro," he said, continuing the charade. He staggered toward a park bench with the unconscious man in tow, and sat him down. The bench was occupied by a couple of concertgoers. When they saw the gigantic Uly dragging a fully grown man toward them, they hurried away. Without further fanfare Uly surreptitiously cuffed the man's wrist to the bench. Uly quickly emptied the suspect's pockets of his phone, wallet, and car keys and drifted off into the crowd. The whole incident had taken seconds and no one in the crowd paid any attention.

One down.

Ashes of the Martyrs

It was weird riding in a police car with all the windows shot out. We were racing toward San Antonio and I kept watching the time on Miss Ruby's phone tick down. The light bar on top of the cruiser was blasted to bits and we got some weird looks from other drivers.

"We have to figure out where they're going to set off the car bomb," Angela whispered to me. "Was there anything you overheard?"

With the windows shot out and the air rushing through the car, it was a little easier to talk without the sheriff hearing us.

"Well, it wasn't like, 'Hey, hostage kid! Guess where we're going to set off the bomb and hopefully kill thousands of people,' " I said quietly.

"This isn't right," the sheriff interjected. "Three people who I thought just lived in my county like regular folks just died. And the president of the United States told me they were terrorists. Now you and Dirk tell me I gotta get you to San Antonio fast, so your parents don't miss you," he snorted. "I

ain't stupid and I wasn't born yesterday. I did two tours in
Iraq. If there're terrorists about, that means an attack of some
kind. Maybe it's a chemical weapon, or a bomb of some kind.
Maybe a truck full of fertilizer. That'd be easy enough to find
around here," the sheriff said. "So you two can just drop the
act. Seems like this Boone fella is being reckless with people's
safety."

Angela and I looked at each other. The sheriff had proven
himself capable and smart. Now we just had to make sure he
didn't change his mind about getting us back to San Antonio.

"I know it appears that way," Angela said, "but he's got a
pretty amazing team of agents working for him. He wants to
catch these people. If they suspect we know about the bomb,
they'll fade away again and we'll never find them. And Boone
is very close to destroying the whole group of them. And if we
get this phone to X-Ray, he might be able to figure out a way
to stop them cold."

"That's all well and good," the sheriff said. "But what if
he's wrong? What if he doesn't catch them? What then?"

"All I can tell you is that in the last few days a lot of bad
stuff has almost happened and Boone has stopped it. . . ."

"If he's so great and knows everything, like you say, how
come he didn't stop the bomb in Washington and the one
at the USS *Cole* Memorial?" The sheriff was getting more
animated the closer we got to San Antonio. It was hard to
blame him.

"The bomb in Washington happened before the president
put Boone in charge of this operation. The *Cole* Memorial
event was allowed to occur, after making sure no people

would be hurt, so the cell wouldn't get suspicious that he was onto them," Angela explained.

The sheriff muttered something unintelligible. I understood why he was upset. Most men in his position probably didn't have to deal with international terrorism right in their backyard.

Angela changed the subject. "Q, did you hear them say anything that might indicate where they planned to attack?" She was insistent.

"Just nonsensical stuff. I heard them say something about 'ashes of the martyrs.' I guess that's some kind of terrorist talk. When they blow themselves up they'll be a bunch of ashes? And I heard . . ." I stopped, thinking over everything I'd heard. "They said something about making sense of a graph," I said. "Could it be some kind of graph of expected casualties . . . or . . . I don't know!"

Angela was quiet. She was concentrating so hard I thought her face might crack.

"Say that again," Angela said.

"What?"

"The graph . . . you said they couldn't make sense of a graph?" she asked.

"Yeah, but they were way across the room and whispering and all I could hear were bits and pieces of what they were saying. I think it's just a bunch of terrorist mumbo jumbo . . ." I said.

"No, it's not! I know where they're going! Give me your phone!" she said.

I handed her the iPhone and she hit the redial to call

X-Ray.

"X-Ray, it's Angela. Q overheard something . . . you need
to get the intellimobile to the Alamo Memorial. Block all the
phone signals! Shut them down. It's not the Alamo itself or the
concert! It's the memorial! Hurry! Tell Boone! X-Ray, listen!
I know that's where they're going . . . we'll be there in ten
minutes." Angela disconnected the call.

"Sheriff, you need to get us to the cenotaph as soon as you
can," she said.

"Sure, why not?" Sheriff Hackett replied. "Probably only
meet up with a whole division of Taliban troops there. No
problem."

I hoped the sheriff was just being sarcastic. Nevertheless
he coaxed the battered car to go faster. It picked up speed and
we were soon barreling down the street in the direction of the
concert. His siren still worked and traffic pulled over as we
flew by.

"Can you fill me in?" I asked her.

"It was in our homework. You said they mentioned 'ashes
of the martyrs.' After the Battle of the Alamo, the bodies of
the slain defenders were burned in a huge funeral pyre near
the mission. Their ashes–the ashes of the martyrs, as the
locals referred to them–were interred at the San Fernando
Cathedral. The style of monument built on the site of the pyre
is sometimes called a cenotaph. That's what you heard. It's got
to be the place where they intend to hit."

"You researched all that stuff?" I said.

"Somebody has to do our homework," she said with a grin.

"Nice." In the midst of a crisis, Angela was still the

homework police.

The cruiser screamed up Houston Street, heading east as we approached the intersection of Alamo Plaza Boulevard. The crowd was thinner now that the concert had begun and the traffic had lightened on the streets near the plaza. But as we drew nearer, Angela and I both saw it at the same time.

A white SUV was coming directly at us from the west. If it reached the intersection it would turn and head directly toward the Alamo Memorial.

With nothing to stop it.

Two to Go

"Boone, it's Vanessa, do you copy?" Vanessa touched the Bluetooth.

"Copy, go ahead," Boone said.

"Where are you?" she asked.

"Toward the front of the crowd, near the stage. Why?"

"I've spotted another suspect. But I've lost Uly. The crowd is really thick here. This guy is a little more on guard. I'm not sure I'll be able to get close enough to–hold on."

There was silence for a moment.

"Vanessa?" Boone said. X-Ray cut in.

"Boone! This is X-Ray. I just got a call from Angela. She's inbound with Q and that sheriff you met earlier. She says the target is the Alamo Memorial. The cenotaph."

"I thought you told them to stay!" Boone yelled.

"I did! But they're coming anyway. I'm moving the intellimobile next to the cenotaph and I'm going to cut all phone signals in that immediate area. You better get back here!"

"Boone, it's Vanessa. Our suspect just pulled something

out of his pocket. Looks like some kind of modified phone. He's east of your location, about two hundred fifty yards from the monument. I don't see Uly. I need a body catcher! If I take him out, the crowd could panic. Boone, what do I do?"

"Felix, can you see anything?" Boone asked, moving toward Vanessa's position. "Do you have a shot?"

"Negative. I can't be sure which man she's eyeballing," Felix said.

"Vanessa, take him. Take him now, as soon as you can! Don't let him use that gadget!"

Boone had been standing beside a tree with a trash bin beside it, the stage to his back. In the next instant he appeared behind Vanessa's target, just as her knife landed in the center of the man's back. Boone removed the knife and, much like Uly did, relieved the man of his phone and drag-walked him to a nearby bench. The man was wearing a dark windbreaker. Luckily, the bloodstain growing on his back was not readily visible. Boone sat him down and checked his pulse to make certain he was gone.

Uly appeared out of the crowd and stood next to Boone.

"I was inside the radius where X-Ray shut down the phones. My headset lost contact," he said.

"No worries. It had to be done this way," Boone said. Vanessa joined them at the bench.

"Now what?" she said.

"You heard X-Ray," Boone said. "Fill in Uly on the way to the cenotaph. Keep a sharp eye. Felix, Uly and Vanessa will try to identify any targets so stay ready. We may need you. Let's move. We've got a bomb to find," he said.

They arrived at the memorial plaza a few moments later. Most of the crowd had moved toward Bonham Street, nearer the Alamo, but there were still far too many people near the target.

"We've got to think of a way to clear some of these people out of here without starting a panic," Boone said into the Bluetooth. "The last thing we want is a stampede where everyone gets crushed."

Off in the distance, parked along Alamo Memorial Boulevard near the cenotaph, they could see the intellimobile with the antenna array extended. Boone knew X-Ray was jamming all phone signals, but he still worried about the drivers detonating the bomb manually.

"What are we going to do?" Vanessa asked. "We can't have Felix fire a couple of warning shots. That will panic everyone."

"I got an idea," Uly said. He tore off his shirt. Like Felix, Uly had been in a lot of scrapes during his time in the CIA, DEA, and Delta Force. His thickly muscled back and chest were covered with scars that made him look like he'd taken on three grizzly bears in a wrestling match and come out on the short end.

Uly mussed his hair and started trotting around in circles, bumping into bystanders while shouting at the top of his lungs, "Who wants to fight? Anybody want to try me? I got a hundred dollars says nobody in this crowd can last more than ten seconds with me! I'll fight you with one hand!" He looked like a wild man, and he slurred his words like a drunk. He started shadowboxing while the crowd around the plaza looked on in confusion and then, as he'd planned, in fear.

"Come on! Who wants a piece of me? I can take you all on! I'll fight anybody!"

The effect was immediate and people moved quickly away from the madman. In less than a minute nearly a third of them had migrated toward the safety of the crowd nearer the stage.

"Vanessa, you watch the street. If the cenotaph is the target, they're coming down Alamo Memorial Boulevard. Felix, you be ready. If they're approaching along Houston we're going to need you," Boone said. He said into the Bluetooth, "X-Ray, do you have eyes on Angela and Q or the SUV yet?"

"Negative, but I was just about to tell you, Boone: Somebody just took down all the traffic cams again. I'm trying to hack in and get them back up but it's happening. They've got to be close!"

The three headed back toward the intersection of Houston Street and Alamo Memorial Boulevard. Boone had a feeling the terrorists would choose the easiest path to the target and this was it. Even with the street closed to through traffic they could crash through the barricades and have an unimpeded path to the cenotaph.

"Boone!" Vanessa shouted.

Boone spun at her shout and saw her pointing toward a white SUV accelerating up Houston Street. It was careening back and forth through the traffic and people in the street scattered and ran as it rolled along.

Boone heard Uly shouting, "Down, down, everybody down!" He lost track of Vanessa, because all of his attention was now focused on a sheriff's car that was accelerating toward the Tahoe from the opposite direction.

It was on a collision course.

The Good Guys

"Sheriff!" Angela shouted, "you've got to stop that SUV!"

"Hang on!" the sheriff yelled. He punched the gas and sped toward the intersection. The Tahoe veered around a car and turned onto Alamo Plaza Boulevard. Angela and I each braced for the impact with one hand while we held onto Croc with the other. Before the Tahoe could accelerate past us, the sheriff's cruiser hit it broadside. All of us, the sheriff included, were screaming at the top of our lungs. Even Croc was howling as the cruiser crossed the plaza, the siren screaming and the sheriff laying on the horn. The two cars were joined together in a mass of twisted metal. They careened down the street, tires and brakes screeching in protest. Pedestrians leaped out of the way and it was a miracle we didn't hit anyone.

The impact spun us around. I looked out of what had been the rear window of the patrol car and saw the face of one of the drivers. There was a look of utter shock in his eyes.

The collision twirled the Tahoe around so that its front end was facing us, and we continued skidding down the street.

We traveled side by side with the SUV for a short distance. Then the sheriff twisted the wheel hard to the left, and the SUV driver hit the Tahoe's brakes. It slowed, but turned so that it was perpendicular to us. We finally stopped a few yards from the monument.

The air bags had deployed and the two men in the Tahoe were momentarily stunned. But seconds later their doors swung open and they staggered out. Both of them carried machine pistols. One of them had a black box with a little metal antenna on it. The sheriff kicked his door open, yelling at us to get down. He jumped out of the car with his revolver drawn. His gun fired twice. I'm pretty sure I heard other shots but couldn't swear to it. It all happened so fast it was difficult to sort out. Then it was quiet for a moment before I heard people shouting, screaming, and running.

Angela and I clambered out of the cruiser. I felt like a brick wall had fallen on top of me. The sheriff stood in front of his battered patrol car. His gun was pointed at the two bodies lying on the ground. My ears were ringing. I remembered Boone and X-Ray saying that the car bombs also had timers on them. I worried this one might have been activated before the sheriff shot the man holding the detonator.

"Run!" I shouted. "Everybody ru–" I was interrupted by the sound of the hatchback door on the SUV opening. Looking around, I found X-Ray's legs hanging out of the back of it. A few seconds later he climbed out holding a bunch of different-colored wires in one hand and a multi-tool in the other. X-Ray had disarmed the bomb.

A crowd was gathering and people were gaping at the two

shattered cars.

X-Ray held up the bundle of wires as if he was showing off a fish he had just caught. "You should know," he said to the crowd, "that this model is being recalled. It's prone to sudden and uncontrollable acceleration." Without another word, he scrambled away and disappeared into the intellimobile.

Angela, Croc, and I walked around to stand behind the sheriff. He still held his gun pointed in the direction of the two men lying on the ground. I wasn't surprised at all to find Boone kneeling next to the two men, checking their pulses.

"You can holster your weapon, Sheriff Hackett," he said. "It's over."

Explanations

Sheriff Hackett returned his revolver to its holster and knelt beside the two bodies. Uly and Vanessa were using their Homeland Security IDs to move the crowd back and away from the scene.

Boone spoke into his Bluetooth. "X-Ray, get J.R. on the phone. Tell him we need a cleanup crew here on the double."

"You going to tell me what happened?" the sheriff asked him.

"You saw what happened, Sheriff," Boone said. "You, Tom Hackett, faithful public servant, took out two terrorists. One shot each, center mass. I saw all the trophies in your office. You're quite a marksman. Not only that but you've just saved countless lives. You're a hero. That's what happened."

"Mr. Boone, I'm a good shot. I don't dispute it. But I see two dead men here. I shot twice and I know I hit them each in the chest. But both of them also have head shots from what looks to be a high-powered rifle. And this fellow here—you'll notice he has a knife sticking out of the side of his neck. I *am* a good shot, but I can't throw a knife worth squat. So again, I ask you, what happened here?"

Boone looked up across the street to the hotel roof. There was no sign of Felix but he knew there wouldn't be. He reached down and removed the knife from the dead man's neck and wiped the blood off on the suspect's shirt.

"Sheriff, I don't see a knife wound. And I'm pretty sure the official autopsy is going to show that both men died from gunshot wounds to the chest from your service revolver. Not a sniper's rifle," Boone said.

"Mr. Boone, I know you have the president on speed dial but I don't know that I can go along with this. I–"

"I'm also quite certain that during your next reelection campaign, you're going to get a visit from a very prominent politician who is going to assist with your fundraising. A politician currently residing at 1600 Pennsylvania Avenue in Washington, D.C. In fact, I'm pretty sure your next election is in the bag," Boone said.

The sheriff stood and looked off into the darkness for a few seconds.

"All right. You can't or won't tell me anything. I don't see how I can make you. But let me tell you something, Mr. Boone, and this may come as a surprise to you. I don't give two hoots about my next election. I care about the law and doing what's right."

"I think that's pretty clear, Sheriff," Boone said.

"Then if you can't tell me everything, you at least owe me something. You need to tell me these two men I just killed were criminals. Tell me these were bad guys. I need to know that at least."

"Sheriff Hackett," Boone said, "they were the worst. Like I said. You're a hero. You did a good thing tonight. You should sleep easy."

Boone stuck out his hand. This time the sheriff shook it with a lot more enthusiasm.

Chicago

The concert was almost over, but Mom and Roger had returned to the stage for an encore. They had opened their set with another single from the album, *Match*, called "What If?" Buddy T. was getting real-time updates that showed the single had already gotten over a quarter of a million downloads from various music sites. It looked like they had another hit on their hands.

Mom and Roger had freaked out a little when they saw our cuts and scrapes, caused by all the glass flying around in the patrol car. Boone took them aside and gave them an explanation that seemed to mollify them. He told them the cuts came from the broken glass of an exploding vegetarian casserole dish we'd overheated in the microwave on the coach. He had taken us to wait there because the hotel was filling up with paparazzi and he wanted us out of there. It was a weak story but Mom and Roger were in full concert mode so they bought it. At least for the time being. I think the fact that it was a vegetarian casserole is what sold Roger.

Heather Hughes was also backstage with us. As usual, she and Buddy T. were arguing over something, which is how they seemed to spend most of their time together. Boone was across the stage, keeping an eye on the roadies. Angela and I were watching our parents sing and listening to the crowd go nuts as their voices harmonized perfectly. It felt incredibly normal. Less than an hour before, I'd thought we were going to die. Instead, here we were. I wondered how long our luck would last.

Boone appeared next to us, asking if we were okay. Once again, it was like he materialized out of thin air. Part of me thought he was doing this on purpose to shake us up. I didn't get a chance to say anything before Angela cornered him.

X-Ray had replaced her smashed phone and all of her texts, e-mail, and photos had been loaded onto the new iPhone. She pulled up the picture P.K. had sent us of a man in a Nazi general's uniform standing in some woods with a dog next to him that was the spitting image of Croc.

"So, Boone. You want to tell us about this?" she asked.

"What about it?"

"Is this you? Did you fight in the Second World War? How old are you? You can't have fought in the Second World War because you'd be in your eighties now. You're old but you're not that old. Or are you? What do you have to say about this? Did you fight against the Nazis? Were you in Buffalo Bill's Wild West Show in 1902?" she demanded.

"Angela, I've fought and been in a lot of places. More than I can remember sometimes," Boone said, suddenly sounding tired.

"Is this you?" Angela waved the picture on her phone in Boone's face. "Is your real name Antonio Beroni? Is that an alias?"

Boone straightened up. "Where did you get that name?"

"Never mind where we got it. Is that your real name or not? And is this you in the picture?" Angela was really getting worked up.

"We're not going to talk about this right now," he said.

"That's what you said last time," she said firmly.

He just shrugged. "Listen. Heather is flying you and your parents and Buddy T. to Chicago. The SOS crew and I are driving the coach and the intellimobile. We're leaving now so we can get a head start on the traffic. I'll see you when you get to Chicago. Since we won't arrive until after you do, don't get any ideas. Pat Callaghan is already there. He's going to stick to you like glue. And I mean it. No tricks. No trying to ditch him. You won't be able to, anyway. But if you go anywhere, he goes with you until I get there. Is that clear?"

We didn't say anything. Angela still wanted answers. She stood there, arms crossed, chewing on her lower lip. I knew she had a lot more to say to Boone but it wasn't going to happen now. My needs were much simpler. I just wanted to never have anyone shoot at me ever again.

"I'll take that as a yes," he said. "C'mon, Croc."

He turned and left us, heading out to where the coach was parked.

"You owe us answers, Boone!" Angela hollered after him. He just waved his arm and kept walking, Croc trailing alongside.

"He's making me really angry," Angela said.

"I know," I said. "But he and Croc have also saved our bacon a couple of times. Maybe we should cut him some slack."

"Or not. Why can't he just tell us who he is, what he's been doing all these years?"

She shook the phone with the picture at me. "I don't care what he says. I'm going to find out who–or what–he is. What are you going to do?" When she was mad, Angela liked to issue challenges. Especially to me.

I had been thumbing through the photographs on Miss Ruby's iPhone. There were dozens of pictures of Chicago buildings and streets. I held the phone up so Angela could see a picture of the Chicago skyline.

"I think we can worry about Boone later. You know how they sent your mom to Chicago? Well, right now, I think we ought to try to figure out why the ghost cell always seems to show up wherever we are."

Roland Smith

Born and raised in Portland, Oregon, Roland Smith was just five years old when his parents gave him an old manual typewriter that weighed more than he did, and he's been writing ever since. Now he is the award-winning author of eighteen novels for young readers and more than a dozen nonfiction titles and picture books for children.

Raised in the music business, Smith decided to incorporate that experience as a backdrop for the *I, Q* series.

When he is not at home writing, Roland Smith spends a good part of the year speaking to students at schools around the country. Learn more about the *I, Q* books at www.iqtheseries.com. Learn more about Roland Smith at www.rolandsmith.com.

Michael P. Spradlin

New York Times best-selling author Michael P. Spradlin has written more than twenty books for children and adults. He is the author of the *Killer Species* series and the international best-selling *The Youngest Templar* trilogy. He lives in Michigan and can be visited on the Web at michaelspradlin.com.

www.IQtheSeries.com